Turnaround

James Asparro

D1707748

James Asparro

ISBN: 9798361520381

Contents

1. Is That All There Is?

The silence, right before the applause, seems like an eternity.

I just played the last furious note of Tchaikovsky's Violin Concerto in D. I can't see the audience because the bright stage lights blind me in the ornate 1928 Arlene Schnitzer Concert Hall. Having family, friends, and strangers show such appreciation is gratifying. I practiced this iconic concerto for years, so I embedded every note and nuance in my brain. It invaded my dreams like some strange spell at Hogwarts. Alex, my awesome violin teacher, knows what it feels like to play this piece. Is it almost like being in love? I feel exhilarated but alone for some odd reason. Something is missing.

Claire Devine emerges from the oboe section and comes toward me. I had never noticed her bright lipstick smile before; it matches her red hair. She hands me a bouquet of roses as she surprises me with a kiss on the cheek. She's also an actress and stars in all our high school plays, including the upcoming play, Brigadoon. Could my childhood buddy be morphing into someone new?

Ann, the stage manager, is signaling me to exit the stage. She tells me to stand here for a spell backstage while they clap. It's a standing ovation, so she pushes me out to take a bow. Eventually, they want an encore. Jenny, the assistant concertmaster, also plays piano, and we had practiced Tchaikovsky's Romance No. 6, "None but the Lonely Heart," in case there was a demand. The stage crew brings out the Steinway grand concert piano while everyone claps. After we play it, I feel even more alone.

They're screaming things at me like, "You kick ass Theo!" and "Joshua Bell would be jealous." Claire's in the back of the room with a movie star smile. She's with my mom, my twin sister Emma, and my stepfather Thomas. Thomas is an outrageous person. I still can't beat his time in solving the Rubik's cube; how could an older guy be cooler than that? He's a billionaire but has plans to give most of his money away to help with the homeless problem in Portland. How my mom snagged him, I'll never know. Everyone says my mom's glamorous. I guess she is, but she's just my mom, Megan Hall—a hospice nurse at the VA. Emma looks a lot like her. She has the same long blond hair. Emma is so interested in astronomy that she doesn't pay much attention to boys, though I can tell they pay attention to her. She only likes intelligent guys. She has a boyfriend, Zach, who plays the guitar.

I follow Ann to the lobby, where hundreds of people are in line to greet me where I must smile and pretend that I'm happy. Alas, a devastated landscape passes by while I am on a train to nowhere. I wave and smile and shake hands, but no one is there. There's a cacophony of sounds in the room.

Then, a guy with a suit stares at me. He hands me his card. It reads, "Michael Townsend, PBS American Prodigies."

He gives me a big smile and says, "Would you like to be on the show?"

"Are you serious?" I ask.

"I flew here from Boston to see you play in person. Your teacher, Alexandria Savich, told me I'd be stupid if I didn't see you perform. She's right. We would love to feature you on our national show."

"Seriously? I need to think about it. How do you know Alex?" I ask.

"I've known her forever. We played in the Boston Youth Symphony together a hundred years ago."

Alex, my violin teacher, walks up and presents herself, "Hi Michael, long time no see. Are you glad you came?"

Townsend says, "Words cannot describe how well this young man performed. He would be a delight to have on our national broadcast."

I think, "I just played a nearly impossible concerto, and PBS American Prodigies want me to play on national television. Why do I feel so disconnected? Something is missing."

They shut down the Arlene Schnitzer Concert Hall, but people still wait in line in the lobby to congratulate me. We all must leave, so I wave to the disappointed people who waited in line. We drive to our home in the First Addition of Lake Oswego. Mom makes some tea for us. We all sit down in the living room. They're looking at me like I should say something.

Emma starts the conversation with, "Do you like any other girls besides good old Claire?"

"Uh, I don't know. I haven't had time to think about it. Why do you ask?"

"I overheard some girls talking in the lobby, and they were crushing on you."

"What did they say?" I ask.

"When Claire kissed you, your face turned the color of the roses she gave you; this was so cute to them, they could hardly contain themselves. They think you're hot."

"Claire's a good friend, but...."

Thomas clears his throat with perfect timing. "Theo, I'm proud of you. It takes incredible effort to focus and work as hard as you did. That's mostly what it takes to succeed in just about everything."

"Thanks, Thomas. That's quite a compliment coming from someone as accomplished as you."

"Oh, I almost forgot." I pulled out the card that the guy from PBS American Prodigies gave me.

"He told me he wants me on the show." I pass the card around.

When Emma sees the card, she exclaims, "Are you shitting us? This will make you nationally famous!"

Mom looks at Emma with a disapproving look. "Stop swearing," she says.

Mom stops to reconsider her criticism and says with wide-open eyes, "You're not shitting us, are you?"

Emma looks at mom smugly.

Thomas has a big smile on his face.

"Something's missing," I say. "Things are just happening too fast. I need to wrap my head around all this." I go to bed totally wiped.

For the first time in months, I dream about a happy place without Tchaikovsky, where I've never been; I've yet to discover this place. Perhaps time and life experience will give me some answers.

2. The Ask

PBS American Prodigies was terrific. I played Dvorak's Romantic Pieces Op. 75 for Violin and Piano. My accompanist was the host of the show. The school recorded it somehow and showed it in every classroom. Everyone in the school was so moved that they wrote me in for senior class president; this is the last thing I want to do. I'm not a politician.

We're having lunch in the high school cafeteria together.

"Fred Freemark asked me to the prom," Claire declares.

As I crunch down on a piece of celery, I ask, "What did you tell him?"

"What do you think, Theo?"

"Uh, you said nothing and just quivered with unexpected excitement."

"Sure, silly. I declined his generous offer."

"How'd he take the rejection?"

"He had this weird look and said to me, 'No girl has ever turned me down. Besides, our parents hang out together. They're members of the Exclusive River Country Club; they go to the same church, and you and I grew up in million-dollar homes—in Dunthorpe. We're destined to be together."

"Sounds rather privileged and entitled," I say.

"He also boasted that he's the captain of the football team and first in line for senior class president."

I add, "Rather arrogant as well."

"This gets even better," she smiles.

"I'm listening."

"I reminded him that everyone I know is writing Theo Hall in for senior class president."

"But I'm not running for it."

"Too bad Theo. You're a star after your performance on national public television."

Then Fred said, "Just because Theo got on national television and stroked his fiddle doesn't mean he should represent the senior class. Theo is from First Addition of Lake Oswego—a rather humble neighborhood. We're from Dunthorpe where, as you know, people of our 'class' live. Also, my mother thinks that we should be dating."

"So, I'm no good because I'm from First Addition?" I ask.

"That's what he said, reflecting how my mother feels too."

"I'm not sure why you kissed me in front of thousands of people at the PYP concert. Your mother must have blown a fuse."

"She not only blew all her breaker switches, but she also had to see her weird pastor to deal with her horrible feelings over my un-Christian behavior."

"Your 'un-Christian behavior' embarrassed me, but I enjoyed it. Who wouldn't enjoy a sweet kiss from a girl like you?"

Claire blushes.

"Also, Theo, through the grapevine, I heard Fred asked his second choice, Ashley Rich, to the prom. Ashley's mom took her to the Washington Square Mall Nordstrom and bought a $700 designer dress with matching shoes and a purse. While they were there, they got manicures and pedicures. My sources also tell me that Ashley worships Fred Freemark and just knew he would ask her to the prom."

Claire asks me pensively, "Theo, have you asked anyone to the prom yet?"

"I wasn't planning to go."

"Theo, will you go to the prom with me?"

"You want to go to the prom with me?"

"Yes, silly goose. Of course, I do. Who wouldn't want to go to the prom with you?"

"Okay, sounds like a plan," I say. "I'd love to go to the prom with my BFF. What would your mom think of us going to the prom together?"

"She'll blow up for several reasons."

Claire puts her hand in the air and starts counting with her index finger:

"One, because your stepfather, Thomas Harrison, is a famous liberal democrat who wants to give stuff to undeserving homeless people with the Emma's Wish Foundation. Two, she hates your church because it supports a woman's right to her own health care decisions, helps LGBTQ people, is pro-Palestine, against the war in Iraq, etcetera."

She pauses for a spell.

"Three, your pastor and your violin teacher wrote a 'blasphemous' book, God in the Numbers, making the New York Times bestseller list. The title alone angers and confuses her all at the same time; she just can't understand how God has anything to do with numbers. Four, she hates your mother because she's a lowly hospice nurse and 'revoltingly glamorous.' Five, your stepfather may become the next Mayor of Portland; she's confident he'll tax the rich and give away her capital gains taxes to undeserving poor people. There's more, but I can't remember them offhand; no pun intended."

Claire likes to keep lists. Even in grade school, she kept lists of everything and would challenge me to remember what was on them.

"Doesn't your mother want the homeless problem fixed in Portland? She could shop more downtown if she didn't have to walk past homeless people."

Claire laughs, puts her index finger up again, and starts counting:

"One, both my parents think homeless people are lazy. If they would just work, they wouldn't be ruining our fair city with ugly tents and piles of garbage everywhere. They don't want their tax dollars going to lazy homeless people."

I respond, "Emma's Wish is a project my stepfather founded to get people off the street and into rehab if they want it. Emma's Wish is half funded by Thomas and half by voluntary donations. Not one tax dollar is going into the project. Because of Emma's Wish, there's a people's campaign to elect my stepfather Mayor of Portland. What do your parents think of this?"

Clare shakes her head as if this doesn't matter to her parents.

"Two, they feel, like libertarians do, that if everyone helped themselves, no one would be needy, and we wouldn't need Emma's Wish. Three, my mother has a copy of Ayn Rand's Atlas Shrugged on her nightstand. She strongly believes, like Ayn Rand, in the virtue of selfishness. Four, my mother is beside herself that I turned down the great Fred Freemark, and will go to the prom with you, a product of the 'democrat communist devil himself.' Five, she clapped when your church burned down and wasn't happy Doctor Dawson survived the fire!"

"She's a heartless piece of work. How'd you guess I'd go to the prom with you?"

"I just knew, you stupid klutz. Since we were ten years old, I've known that we would go to the senior class prom together. I have several reasons for this. One...."

"Stop—no more lists. I give up. Should we pick you up at your house if your mom hates me so much?"

"No. I'm getting ready at your house. It will thrill your mom to help me prepare for the senior class prom, because she loves me. We've already made plans to do this."

"So, you just assumed that I'd say yes, and you already made plans to get ready at my house?"

"Theo, someday you'll understand."

"Wow, I'm sorry it's so difficult for you because of me and my family."

"Wrong," Claire states emphatically, "Your parents are cool. My parents are weird."

The lunch period ends, and we must return to our classes.

3. Math

When trigonometry class is over, I see Emily Young sitting on the floor in the room's corner, crying. She's a nice girl, so I can't understand why she doesn't appear to have many friends at school. I stop and talk to her on my way out.

"You okay?"

"It's nothing."

"Yeah, sure; you're sitting in the corner on the floor, not looking so happy."

"You wouldn't understand, Theo. Trig is easy for you. You don't seem to pay much attention in class, yet you get A-pluses on all your tests. You have impressed everyone in the school with your violin, were on national television, and you seem to breeze through trig. You're disgusting."

"Disgusting? Look, Emily, you can do anything if you know the basics and concentrate. Music is a lot like trig. If you need some help, ask me."

I sit down on the floor next to her.

"I got a C-minus on this test and am planning to quit trig. I don't need all this crap."

Tears run down her face.

"May I look at it?"

"Well, nothing could be more embarrassing, but be my guest."

She shrugs her shoulders and hands me the test. I can see where she needs some help to put her on top of things.

"Do you have a few minutes? Let's go to the library. I think I can help you out."

I finally see her smile.

"Really? You'd help me out?"

"Sure."

Emily walks with me to the library. She's taller than me and somewhat frumpy, but Emily's the sweetest person. I feel comfortable around her because she isn't so made up all the time—like the rally squad girls. She just has this no-nonsense way that I like, and she's real.

We walk past Fred Freemark, captain of the football team, and his football buddies; Fred blurts out, "Hey Fiddle Head, got yourself a big new squeeze? Why, she looks as fit as a fiddle." All his friends laugh.

"Ignore him," I say to Emily.

"I'll try," she timidly replies.

We keep walking.

"He can't stand that you're being written in to be senior class president when you're not even running for the position."

"I don't want to be the senior class president."

When we get to the library, after she settles down, I help her with some math basics, like the order of operations; this was fouling her up. We go over them several times. It finally clicks for her why she got a C-minus on the test. She just needed to get the order of operations straight—back to the basics.

She still appears to be upset, so I ask, "Is something else bothering you besides Fred Freemark and your trig test?"

"Theo, you wouldn't understand; I'm just having a bad day."

"Try me."

Emily appears to be timid. I couldn't tell. She just sits there pondering her alternatives.

Finally, she says, "Theo, I have told no one this, but my parents are going through a divorce. It's a long and complicated story."

"I'm listening."

Emily seems reluctant but asks, "Scout's honor, you won't tell anyone?"

"My lips are sealed, I swear."

"Okay, you asked for it. My dad is a software engineer, and my mom's a Zumba instructor. She fell in love with a woman in her class and now lives with her. I live with my dad in the great big house I grew up in. He sits around moping when he's not at work. We both miss her, but she's gone. They haven't divorced yet, so she's, weirdly enough, living with a woman. They will finalize the divorce soon."

There's an uncomfortable pause.

I take a deep breath and figure if she can spill the beans, so can I.

I blurted out, "My parents went through a divorce too."

"Seriously? I assumed everything in your family was perfect—like you. How'd it end?"

I clear my throat, "My father is a naval officer and a world-class chess whiz. All I know is that my father wasn't an angel overseas, and my mom divorced him. I think it's much more complicated than this, but this is all I know."

She's listening intently, and the tears are gone from her face.

"My father will soon be an Admiral in the Navy. Rarely does anyone outsmart him, including our enemies, so he keeps getting promoted. He's the captain of a navy ship now, deployed somewhere in the Far East. When mom and dad divorced, it was a big cluster bomb."

I didn't tell her the whole revolting story. I knew more about the divorce than my mom thought I knew.

"Wow," Emily utters. "How do you cope with it?"

"You just have to deal with it as best as possible."

"How do I do that?"

"I asked my pastor the same question. He told me, 'You can let what others say destroy your life or realize that life is what you make of it, and that is all in your hands.'"

Emily looks at me with wet eyes. "So, I should just suck up my feelings, realizing that my life is in my hands?"

"Yup."

"I'm mortified about my mom running away with a woman. I know times are more accepting of gay people, but I never suspected my mom's a lesbian."

"You didn't run away; your mom did."

I sense that Emily's thinking about it from her mom's perspective.

"My mom loves me—that I'm certain of. She always tells me this. She told me that even though she was leaving my father, she loves me as much as she ever did."

"Think about this, Emily: Your mom was there for you when you grew up and wants to be there for you now. But she's a person with feelings, and needs, just like you. She's not perfect either. Try to accept her life choices and respect her for the bold decision she must have made. She didn't do it to hurt you. You had nothing to do with it. You'll never know what goes on between your parents. She fell in love with another woman. Stuff happens."

"I still don't respect her for this. Love is a choice. My father's a way-cool guy. Couldn't she just control her passions and live up to her marriage commitment? She's always so controlling. She disapproves of any girl my weird brother dates and is always on my case for even thinking about going on a date."

I don't know what else to say, so I think of something that may help her sort through things. "Emily, you need someone to talk to. I feel somewhat honored that you'd trust me with all this, but I'm not very experienced with this stuff. One person could help you deal with your situation."

"Who's that?"

"My pastor, Dr. Ben Dawson. He helped me with my feelings about my parent's divorce."

Emily finally smiles, "Oh, so Dr. Dawson's your pastor? He taught the class 'How the Bible Has Shaped History' when I was a junior. He's a smart and great guy. Most of the girls in the class took it not because they were interested in how the Bible has shaped history, but because they all had a crush on Dr. Dawson."

"Why's that?" I ask.

Emily smiles again, "Well, gee whiz Theo, haven't you noticed? He's cute, smart, witty, funny, and a hunk. Even his cargo pants are cool."

I laugh. "I never thought of him that way."

"Do I just call him?"

"Yes. Call him at the Lake Oswego Progressive Church of America and make an appointment. Tell him I sent you."

"Will do," Emily says.

4. The Prom

On prom night, Thomas drops us off in his Tesla in front of the Tiffany Center in downtown Portland. Claire's wearing a simple spaghetti strap black dress with black pumps, a pearl necklace, and pearl earrings. My mother must have braided some of her long red hair—the rest tumbles down on her bare shoulders. Deep inside, I'm conflicted. Is this the same girl I went to grade school with? She's still ten years old in my mind, like a sister, but starting to look like a woman. She plays Fiona MacLaren in the musical Brigadoon at school. It's scheduled for five performances next week.

I ask her, "How are the rehearsals of Brigadoon going? I look forward to seeing you in the play."

Smiling, she says, "You'll know it when you see it." She's strangely quiet about any details.

The orchestra playing in the ballroom is called, "Carl Smith and the Natural Gas Company." I'm not a jazz musician, but these musicians can play well. Carl Smith has been around for so long in Portland that his music repertoire goes way back many years. They play all the old standards that I love from the forties to the present. I could never in a million years improvise as they can. I'm a classical musician; we don't improvise. We just play what someone else has written. When the alto saxophone player plays A Portrait of Jennie from the 1948 movie and then improvises on the chords, I can't believe his intonation and phrasing. While improvising, he anticipates chord changes as if they're implanted in his head. I'm overwhelmed with the music and, perhaps because of Claire, other new other new emotions? Nah, she's still a little girl—always in my face.

Fred and Ashley are at the punchbowl. Fred is pouring some alcohol in it from a flask hidden by his coat jacket. His football buddies think they're hiding him from view when there's a big ceiling mirror where I can see what he's doing. Ashley looks like something out of Vogue Magazine. Fred looks dapper wearing his tailored tux and his $4,000 one-of-a-kind salmon pink Air Jordans. Ashley looks at him like he's a God to be worshiped. Ashley keeps trying to talk to Fred, but he can't keep his eyes off us and completely ignores her. Claire gets involved with drama students as a group of music students surround me. Fred's eyes are laser-focused on Claire when Ashley abruptly walks away from him with tears in her eyes; he doesn't even notice. She gets on the elevator headed to the ground floor, where the front doors are. I run down the stairs and meet her in the lobby. She's on her phone.

I ask her, "Are you okay?"

"I just called for a taxi. I'm leaving. Fred can't keep his eyes off Claire. He should have asked her to the prom."

I don't tell her he did just that.

"You're too good for him, Ashley."

"I am?"

"You sure are. Look, Ashley, you went to a lot of trouble getting all dressed up for the prom. The senior prom only happens once in your life. Don't leave because of a jerk like Fred. Hang out with your friends. Many, if not most, came to the prom without dates, so I'm sure they'd love to spend some time with you."

The taxi pulls up. I give the driver his due.

"Claire and I think you look terrific. However, we also think that dress makes you look like a Hallmark movie actress."

Ashley kisses me on the cheek and says, "Claire's the luckiest girl on earth that you asked her to the prom. I'll be voting for you for class president. Fred Freemark is toast."

I didn't tell her that Claire had asked me to the prom.

"Don't worry about your ride home. We'll take you home."

Her tears are gone, and she walks back into the prom determinately with a devilish smile on her face.

I walk back into the room, and Claire, with her male counterpart from Brigadoon, sings with the orchestra, "It's Almost Like Being in Love." I'm blown away by their compatibility as performers. Even their vibratos are in sync. Claire's voice carries like an opera singer. The senior class goes berserk. I've never heard her sing like this.

When she walks off the stage, she's surrounded by students. Finally, when I get to talk to her, she hugs me.

"Where were you?" she asks. "I thought you were going to miss the surprise."

"I'll tell you about that in a second. Did Carl Smith's orchestra just have that 'It's Almost Like Being in Love' arrangement in their charts?"

"No, silly. When the prom committee used Carl Smith and the Natural Gas Company, they did it to have me and my male counterpart in Brigadoon sing one of its songs with the orchestra. We had a rehearsal, with the score from the musical, in Carl Smith's basement at his home. He's offered me a permanent gig with his orchestra."

"Are you going to do it?"

"If I can fit Carl Smith's orchestra in with college, perhaps so, but college comes first."

"You sounded spectacular. You kept all this from me. Where did you get that operatic voice?"

"You haven't been paying attention, Theo. I've been taking voice lessons from a performer in the Portland Opera."

This all slipped by me. I've been so self-centered that I failed to realize that Claire has been working and practicing as hard as me— if not harder.

Claire continues, "We kept this entire performance from everyone. It was a total surprise. This isn't the only reason I asked you to the prom, but one of them. So, where were you at the beginning of the performance?"

"It's a long story. I'm sure Ashley will tell you all about it later. Just make sure we take her home." Claire smiles knowingly.

Fred's worshippers surround him, and he hasn't even noticed that Ashley isn't with him but with her many friends. The prom is nearing an end. Claire asks Ashley if she wants a ride home. A big smile comes across Ashley's face, and she follows Claire and me to the elevators that lead to the exit where Thomas is waiting in his car.

Since Fred has his eyes on Claire and accidentally sees Ashley walk out with us, he runs up to us and, with his hand, stops the elevator doors from closing and barks at Ashley, "Where do you think you're going?"

She calmly replies, "None of your stinking business. Now back off, bucko, and go back to your football fans."

As the elevator door closes, Fred stands there with an expression that looks like a spoiled child who didn't get an ice cream cone. Ashley giggles in delight in the elevator, and we give her high fives.

We get in Thomas's car. He looks at Ashley and asks, "Who do I have the pleasure of meeting?"

I say, "This is Ashley Rich, and she needs a ride home."

Thomas just nods his head asking no questions.

After dropping them off, when we're alone, Thomas finally comments, "Theo, I take you to the prom with one attractive woman and bring you home with two attractive women. Was Emma right, after your Tchaikovsky performance, about you having to fight the women off?"

"Thomas, it's not like that. Ashley had a problem with Fred Freemark, and Claire's just good old, always there, Claire."

5. Freezing Rain

The high school orchestra just finished playing at a mini concert in the auditorium. I have to play in the High School orchestra, because Portland Youth Philharmonic requires it of all their musicians. The high school orchestra uniform includes ridiculous-looking white pants for everyone. I have my black loafers on. I put the polish on them this morning but didn't have time to brush them, so black shoe polish rubbed off on my pants. Claire thought it was hilarious when she saw me sitting in the front row with shoe polish all over my white pants.

After the performance, the orchestra members want me to play something cool. They all saw me on PBS American Prodigies but haven't heard me play anything other than orchestra parts in person.

"Okay," I say. "Here's something I practice to sharpen my chops before a performance."

I play for them a very difficult classical etude that uses most of the various skills needed to get me ready for a performance (Turnaround readers can hear this etude, and many other special effects in the Audible version of this book).

"Wow, Theo, that was outrageous!"

They all clap and pound their feet.

On the same day as the mini concert, I promised Emily another math lesson in the library during the last period when Emily and I are scheduled for study hall. She's picking up on all things math faster than me. In fact, she's giving me lessons on how to do things faster and better. She's exceptional. She doesn't need me anymore for math lessons, as she is way ahead of me. When we're done, we walk to the school's main entrance and wait for the bus.

We see Fred Freemark and his football buddies laughing as they walk toward the exit where we're standing.

Emily says in a low voice, "I can't stand football. It's a brutal and boring sport."

"Concur," I say.

Fred turns on his boom box at full volume playing old fashioned heavy metal hard rock music. It's obnoxious and aimed at Emily and me. From who knows what, Fred's father is wealthy. Fred's father gives him money to buy anything he wants. Fred has an old vintage MG and parades around in it like he's some kind of rock star. He's wearing his one-of-a-kind $4,000 salmon pink Air Jordans today. He doesn't wear them playing football, as he doesn't want them to get them dirty. The Neanderthals come up to Emily and me as Fred turns up the volume on his boombox.

He yells over the noise, "Hey, Fiddlehead, how's it going?"

I don't even look at him or respond, as this would acknowledge his insult. No one ignores Fred Freemark; he doesn't like this at all.

Fred sneers, "What's the matter, Fiddlehead; can't you speak?"

I say to him, "You're looking at me. Are you talking to me, or is there someone named Fiddlehead here?"

I see several students gathering around who hear the exchange.

I ask more loudly above the heavy metal garbage so everyone can hear, "Does anyone here go by the name of Fiddlehead?"

Most of the students are silent.

They don't want to challenge the football team captain and a senior class president contender, so I say, "Fred if you're addressing me, my name is Theo."

Emily finally says to Fred, "You're a pig. Your heavy metal music is an assault on normal people meant for brutal football thugs like you. You can't go around insulting people by calling them stupid names. There's something wrong with you."

I see several students agreeing with her by nodding their heads.

Fred ignores Emily's comment and says to me, "Hey, Fiddlehead, is this your number two squeeze?" He looks Emily up and down, then continues, "There's a lot of her to squeeze, but I thought Claire Devine was your main squeeze?"

I feel like hitting him with my fist, so I hit him with words instead, "Look, Fred, I don't have a beef with you. But I don't like it when you insult me and others. If you think the only reason women exist is for you to 'squeeze' them, then you're a misogynist. You probably don't even know what that word means. You should find a dictionary and look it up. Why don't you back off and play a touch football game? Your brain will last longer this way. Perhaps you should try to read one of the books in your backpack; I'm sure your teachers would be thrilled."

Most of the students gathered around agree with me. The only ones who are on Fred's side are his football buddies. He's being abandoned by most students and backs off.

Fred huffs resignedly, "We'll see you around, Fiddlehead."

I see Fred go outside, followed by his football minions.

Emily says to me, "You're a peach, Theo."

"You have a great way with words too, Emily."

Claire is standing on top of the staircase. "You two are outstanding," she says. "I saw the entire exchange."

All the students around me chant, "Theo for President, Theo for President."

They also most embarrassingly chant, "Theo Rocks, Theo Rocks."

Fred and his friends look defeated as the chants rise above the awful music coming from his boombox.

When we open the main doors of the school to catch the school bus, freezing rain pelts down like pitchforks and hammer handles; everything is covered in a solid sheet of ice. Claire's wearing animal print flats that wouldn't hold very well on the ice. Emily's wearing winter snow boots. I have my unpolished, shoe polish-only loafers on. I'm concerned that Claire might slip on the ice, so I let her hold my arm while I hold onto the rail tightly. As I take the first step, I trip on something I don't see and slide down the stairs; Claire slides with me.

Claire and I end up at the bottom of the stairs and keep sliding toward an oncoming school bus. We're now sliding on the parking meridian; I see the sewer drain, and to brace the sliding, I grab the sewer drain grate with my left hand. It stops me, but I see Claire sliding toward the bus. As she passes by, I grab her coat with my right hand and hold on tight to keep her from ending up in the street in front of the bus; her weight tears something in my left arm. I feel excruciating pain. As it all happened in a few seconds, the bus passes by, oblivious to what happened; it drives over my violin and crushes it to pieces. It would have been Claire had I not held on to her coat. I'm lying in the gutter, with my left hand and wrist twisted and hurting like hell.

Claire gets up, shaken. I ask her, "Are you okay?"

"I'm fine," she answers.

"Are you okay?" she asks.

"I don't know. My left wrist. It's painful. I can hardly move my hand."

Claire calls my mother, who arrives in about half an hour. She must drive slowly because of the slippery and dangerous roads. When we get into the car, Claire explains what happened to my mom. My registered-nurse mom takes one look at my wrist, gets out of the car, finds a plastic bag in the trunk, stuffs a ton of snow in it, and wraps it around my arm. She then drives to the emergency room at St. Vincent Hospital. It takes about an hour with the traffic and the ice. We must wait for another hour. The snowpack helps with the swelling, but my arm and wrist throb in pain. Finally, we're escorted to a waiting room. A doctor comes into the room. She looks at my arm and asks, "What happened to you? Aren't you the talented violinist I saw on television?"

"That's me. I slipped on some stairs and took a fall."

"If you broke something, we'll need to get some x-rays."

I broke no bones, after getting the x-rays, but damaged several tendons. The doctor put bandages on the parts of my arm that scraped the cement curb above the sewer grate. She instructs me I should never even try to play the violin until there's no pain. She tells me that any attempt to play would only worsen the sprain and prolong the healing.

Claire's crying. "Why are you crying?" I ask. "Are you in any pain?"

"I'm okay, but you're not. When you hurt, I hurt. Besides, you saved my life."

My mom asks with great concern, "He did what?"

"Had Theo not grabbed me as I slid toward an oncoming school bus, it would have killed me."

My mom hugs Claire.

Mom says, "I'm glad you're okay, Claire. Theo, you will never cease to amaze me."

I don't know what to say. All I did was what I had to do. When we leave the hospital, I'm bandaged with a sling and a prescription for painkillers. I was supposed to play a PYP concert the following day. I call the conductor of PYP and tell him what happened. He doesn't ask many questions; his only emotions are for music. He says he'll call Jenny, the assistant concertmaster, to be the concertmaster for the rest of the season.

I am out, kaput, damaged. My life will change forever.

6. April Sunshine

Cute little April Ann Dawson is transfixed by the plastic things hanging from her battery-operated swing that I just bought her for her first birthday. She calms down, and we can have a few minutes of peace when she's in her swing.

"Alex, isn't it cool that this swing can calm her down?"

"Ben, remember when she was lying on the floor next to the speakers when we brought her home from the hospital a year ago?"

"Sure do. I still spend many hours on the floor with her."

"Do you notice how calm she is now?" she says.

"Of course, we can talk, and she's happy with her new automatic swing we don't have to push."

Alex looks at me with that, "I know something you don't know," look on her face. She takes April out of her swing, and she's just as calm but crawls over to the speakers. Her eyes are wide open, and she concentrates on the music.

Alex gloats, "When she was just a few days old, I put on a recording of Vivaldi's 'Four Seasons,' and she calmed down like she is now."

"Sounds like Vivaldi's 'Four Seasons' is playing now. So, it's not my cool battery-operated swing that has calmed her down?"

"Perhaps," Alex replies. "But watch this."

Alex goes to the stereo and turns on some country western music on the radio.

April not only crawls away from the music, but she gets up on her legs for the first time and runs away from the speakers. Her first steps are to run away from country-western music. She comes over to me and lifts her arms for me to hug her. This I do with great enthusiasm, as she doesn't always do this. She covers her ears as I hold her.

"Now watch this," Alex says.

She turns Vivaldi back on.

April Sunshine squirms to get out of my arms and walks, not crawls, toward the speakers. She sits on the floor, beaming with happiness and claps her hands to the Four Seasons.

7. Honey and Me

Since our church burned down, the reformed Jewish congregation we hosted for many years is now hosting us. They purchased a former daycare center that was vacant for ten years and turned it into a synagogue. They plan to build a sanctuary on the property but are currently meeting in a simple open space. Spiritually, their reformed Jewish congregation is much like our progressive Christian church. We both look at our religious heritage, considering the historical milieu in which they wrote scripture, and attempt to understand it with our current scientific understanding of the world. We became close congregations. They're thrilled to help us out as we helped them grow to where they could get their own place to gather and worship. They gave me an office in the basement, which perfectly suits me. I like underground living. It makes me feel like a privileged rat.

Joan buzzes me. "Ben, your ten o'clock appointment is here for you."

Maxx Maxwell from the Patriot Guard Riders called an hour ago and wants an emergency appointment with me. He walks into my office, wearing riding leathers, holding two helmets.

"What can I do for you, Maxx?"

"Ben, Johnny Dove died yesterday."

I'm silent for a while.

Finally, I say, "Johnny? I'm so sorry. How'd it happen?"

"He died in his sleep from a heart attack."

"I was just getting to know him," I say.

"He was a special guy," Maxx says.

"This is very sad. Tell me what's going on in your head."

"As you know, Johnny and I got married fifteen years ago. We both served in Iraq together, back when Clinton's 'Don't Ask, Don't Tell' policy was in effect. We met each other because we're both from Portland and got to know each other well. When we got out, we moved back to Portland and got married. Portland's a liberal city, where we're accepted and not discriminated against."

I counter with, "Portland's somewhat liberal, but the rest of Oregon is more conservative. There are certain conservative groups in Portland that are changing this perception. Bad stuff is happening everywhere."

"I know. It's hard being gay anywhere. As you know, the Patriot Guard Riders are at your church for several reasons. We're here because your church saved Charlie Eaton's life. He served honorably in Korea, was all alone after his wife, May, died, and was ready to kill himself, but he found a church that embraced him with love. That's how we all got involved in your church. Johnny loved it here. He loved your sermons as they spoke to him. We find this congregation a refuge and a community of hope and acceptance. This congregation doesn't discriminate against LGBTQ folks. We can all come here and feel accepted and have community. The Patriot Guard Riders honor all Vets; we show up, sometimes when no one else does.

"But besides my grief, I have some good news for you."

"Me?"

"Yes, you, Ben. Johnny left his Harley in his will to you. He knew he had a bad heart and drew up a will several months ago. He left everything else to me."

"Why'd he give his Harley to me?"

"Because he said you look and act like a closeted biker."

"I wonder why he thought this. What am I supposed to do with it?"

"Ride it, you dumbass! Sorry, you're the only minister I could call a dumbass because you're a real dumbass if you don't ride that bike and hopefully honor some deserving veterans with us."

"I used to own a motorcycle in seminary. I drove it everywhere. It was nothing like a Harley, though. Alex would freak out. She thinks motorcycles are unsafe."

"You only live once. You may as well enjoy the thrill of the road. Can you play hooky for a few minutes? I'll drive you to my house where Honey lives."

"Who's Honey?"

"She's your new mistress. You can drive her home."

Maxx gives me a helmet, and we drive his motorcycle to his house, which, ironically, is on the same street I grew up on—Southeast Hawthorne Blvd.

"Maxx, I grew up a few houses down from yours. Mt. Tabor was my backyard when I was a kid."

"So, the great Rev. Dr. Dawson has humble roots?"

"Yup."

Maxx pulls into the driveway of his humble home. He opens the garage door and there stands Honey. She's even painted the color of honey.

"How does it work?" I ask Maxx.

He wheels her into the driveway and shows me everything about her. I start her up, and she makes a growling sound—like a mad dog.

"Just let her warmup," Maxx says, "She'll purr as smooth as honey in a few minutes."

Sure enough, she purrs like a happy cat after warming up to a slow idle. I don't like internal combustion engines, but Honey deserves respect because she's beautiful and was Johnny's old flame. I'm in love.

"Sign this, and she'll be yours. You'll have to go to the DMV and register her in your name."

I thank Maxx, tell him I had better see him in church on Sunday, and wave off. I take it easy on the way home and avoid the freeway. My cargo pants are thick enough to buffer the wind, but I need some riding leathers if I take a fall; I'll get them later. I pull into the synagogue parking lot, get off the bike, and walk into the building. Joan sees me pull in.

"Why Ben, I never knew you were a biker; you look so.... so cool."

"Johnny Dove died," I lament to Joan.

"Johnny?"

"Yup, good old Johnny Dove died. He willed his Harley to me."

She cries and falls into my arms.

Alex walks in. She came to the synagogue to practice a violin piece she will play with the choir. This is absolutely the worst thing that could ever happen. Alex is jealous of any woman who even looks at me. I'm with Joan, my long-time secretary, crying in my arms. Alex has this "I'm going to kill you" look on her face.

"It's.... it's not what you think, Alex. Johnny Dove died."

"Johnny?"

"Yup, good old Johnny Dove died."

Alex cries too, and I have two women crying in my arms. After they calm down, I tell them about Johnny's gift.

Alex snaps out of her tears, "Motorcycle? You own a motorcycle?"

Sheepishly I say, "I drove her here from Maxx's house."

Inwardly, it was ecstasy. I'll have to do whatever it takes to convince Alex that I need this bike for my sanity.

"Let me try her out for a few days and see where it goes. Perhaps we'll go on a ride together sometime?"

Alex looks at me like I'm out of my mind. "Yeah, sure. Me, on a motorcycle, would be like you sitting in a rocking chair, watching a Hallmark movie—knitting."

I had to think of something fast, as I love Honey and want to get to know her. It would be a tremendous insult to Johnny if I don't try Honey. He loved her and wanted me to know her as he did.

I take a bold plunge into never-never land here, "I know you've been attempting to get me to knit for a long time, because you think knitting would be a good outlet for me."

I have avoided this "outlet" like the plague.

"But, if you get on Honey with me, just once, I'll learn how to knit."

I can't believe these words came out of my mouth.

"You will learn to knit if I ride your loud, disgusting motorcycle with you?"

"Yep," I stupidly said. "I'll even watch a Hallmark movie with you."

Alex finally laughs as her jealousy turns to joy.

Joan chimes in enthusiastically, "I'll teach him how to knit. I knitted the sweater I'm wearing."

Alex's smile turns to that "hell no" look. What a conundrum we find ourselves in. On the one hand, Alex would have to ride on a motorcycle, something she vowed never to do. She'd also have to suffer from the possibility that Joan would spend more time with me than was comfortable for her. I would have to learn how to knit, which would be the most painful thing I could think of. Pile on a Hallmark movie and a rocking chair, and I may as well rub salt and vinegar into my wounds.

I offer a temporary solution to the immediate problem. "Why don't I get used to the bike so you will feel more comfortable riding with me before considering taking a ride. I'll do this before Joan teaches me to knit."

Well, this seemed to suit Alex because she didn't want to ride the bike and didn't want Joan to spend more time with me. I feel like I dodged a bullet with my brilliant plan. I have some spectacular plans for Honey and me. The first will involve poor Theo.

8. Lima Bean Wisdom

After the disaster, I live primarily in my room and don't go to school. Losing my ability to play the violin is, to me, like death. I'm having a hard time coping with it. My mom brings me food. I've been living like this, in my room, since the accident—missing the high school graduation ceremony. It thrilled Fred Freemark to be in the spotlight as the captain of the football team and the senior class president. The school graduated me, even though I missed all the final exams. I was a straight-A student from the time I was a freshman. They knew I had my pick of any college in the country as my Scholastic Aptitude Test score was sixteen hundred. From what I've heard, out of the two million students who take the test every year, only about five hundred get the highest possible SAT score— one of those was me. Thomas helped me so much; he taught me to concentrate before doing anything and never give up. I have to do something other than the violin. Juilliard, Curtis, Berklee, and Yale School of Music, all the top ten music schools, offered me full-tuition scholarships. I can't take advantage of them because I can't play the violin anymore. I sit in my room, defeated and depressed. Now I am haunted by daymares. I dream of playing the violin as well as Alex, only to awaken to my arm and wrist pain. I call these "daymares."

Sitting in my room, feeling sorry for myself and haunted by another daymare, I hear the doorbell.

Mom yells, "Theo, you have visitors."

"Who?" I yell back.

"Emily Young and Natalie Schrunk," my mom replies.

Emily's plowing ahead with math, and Natalie, a good friend, is transgender. She 'came out' at our church, much to the shock of her parents. They finally accepted her for who she is, and she's actively involved in the theater arts program at school. She played the supporting role of Charlie Dalrymple in Brigadoon. Emily and Natalie came to the prom together.

Natalie says, "Theo, you can't just sit in your room. Without your support, I wouldn't have had the courage to come out of the closet. Nor would I have had the courage to ride my bike to Dickhoff's church at night and deface their stupid sign."

Emily chimes in, "It was brilliant that after the words 'IF YOU'RE TIRED OF SIN, COME IN,' you wrote in bright red lipstick, 'IF NOT, DIAL 503-555-1125.' It made the newspaper, which started Pastor Dickhoff's public downfall, although his church still supports him. Several days later, on the front page of the Lake Oswego Review, there was a picture of the sign with Natalie's handiwork on it. The headline read, 'Sinful Church in Lake Oswego Removed from the Oregon Interdenominational Coalition Due To Illegal Practice Of Gay Conversion Therapy.' It was insanely satisfying to see this headline."

It's the first laugh I've had since the accident. Every day after that, I have a visitor or two or three. I decide to go ahead and not turn them all away, even though I want to be left alone.

Charlie Eaton brought Lizzy, the wonder dog, to console me. I gave Lizzy to him a few years ago to help with his Post Traumatic Stress Disorder. He was in the hurt locker from losing his wife and all that he suffered during the Korean War.

Charlie says, "Theo, I can sense that you need Lizzy right now, and Lizzy needs you. I'm doing well. The older ladies at our church won't leave me alone. I haven't had to cook lately, as there's always something delicious in the refrigerator from all my female visitors. They do so much cleaning that my house smells like flowers all the time. You need Lizzy more than I do right now."

"Seriously?" I question.

"Let's leave it up to Lizzy. Watch this:" He walks out of my room, calls for Lizzy, and she won't come. She just stays by my side.

"See, you need Lizzy now, and she can tell you need her. I know what it feels like to be wounded and left in a ditch to die. Lizzy understands and knows how to pull you out of a ditch."

Later, Lizzy gets me outside to walk her, and she doesn't give a shit if I could play the violin or not. She just loves me with no strings attached. She stays with me all the time—like a watchdog.

Nadia Jama, part of our church-sponsored family from Ethiopia, comes to visit me. She knows discrimination firsthand. She and Lizzy had many happy moments together. With her nose for suffering and exceptional dog wisdom, Lizzy pulled her out of her shell when she first arrived. I feel terrible about all she went through in Ethiopia, and the discrimination she and her family have endured in the United States, but Lizzy saved her from all her fears.

She sees Lizzy for the first time in several years. "Lizzy!" she screams with pleasure. Lizzy licks her hand, and Nadia sheds a tear.

She holds Lizzy's face with both hands and says to her, "I love you, Lizzy. Without your help, I would still be hiding under a chair."

Lizzy licks her ear. She giggles and laughs.

"Theo, if you need anything, my family and I are here just as you and your church were for us."

The next day, Carla Furbee comes with Detective Jeremy Smith. They hold hands the whole time they're here. This is just plain weird. Carla, Alex's best friend, plays oboe in the Boston Symphonic.

"Theo," says Carla, "I gave Claire Devine a few oboe lessons. She's a stellar musician and a wonderful girl. You're so lucky to have her as a friend."

I come out of my bubble for a second and say, "You should hear her sing. Claire played the starring role in Brigadoon and sang 'It's Almost Like Being in Love' at the senior class prom. In the school play, she brought the house down. She plays the oboe, sings, acts, and dances. She'll probably end up in the movies someday."

Carla has a knowing smile on her face. Jeremy's thrilled to see Lizzy, as Lizzy helped him identify the arsonist who burned down our church.

"Lizzy," says Jeremy, "You can help me solve crimes any day. Your nose for news is terrific. If you ever need a job as a police dog again, just let me know."

Alex and Ben come to visit the next day. I sit on the bed. I look terrible. My hair is getting long, and my 18-year-old sparse Scandinavian facial hair looks ridiculous. Ben sits on a wooden chair. He looks uncomfortable. Alex sits on the floor. I know Ben has a sore butt from his bullet wound, so I throw him a pillow he gratefully uses to sit on. He was escorting a woman to an abortion clinic, and a forced birther shot him. Later, I surmised correctly that the woman Ben was accompanying was my mother. Ben was the only person she could trust at the time with her terrible dilemma. He says nothing. He just sits there. We all stare at each other for an interminable amount of time.

I finally say, "Life sucks."

Ben replies, "Can I tell you a story?"

"Sure."

"I took a botany class in college. We experimented with a lima bean. We pushed it down the side of a glass and watched it grow. The stem went up, and the root went down. My professor turned the lima bean upside down where the stem faced down, and the root faced up. The stem did a U-turn and started growing up again. The root also did a U-turn and grew down again. He kept doing this over and over. At the end of the semester, the little lima bean did countless U-turns. The professor said that the lima bean would continue doing U-Turns until it would run out of nutrients in the soil and die."

"So, are you telling me I need to be like a lima bean?"

"Basically," Ben agrees.

"My wrist hurts too much. I'm not sure I have any nutrients left in me to do any U-Turns."

"Be patient," Ben says.

Alex is responsible for the violin player I am today. She can play the Paganini Caprices faster than a hummingbird can flap its wings without thinking about it. She's the most intelligent person I know.

She says earnestly, "How are you, Theo?"

I'm irritated with all the attention.

I say slowly, "I guess I won't need a violin teacher anymore."

"Theo, I know a talented violinist named Julie DeLeo who graduated from St. Olaf—the same college I attended. Julie is from Portland. Like you, she was in the Portland Youth Philharmonic and graduated from Lake Oswego High School. After college, she moved home to think about her future. All of her college friends were in Minnesota, so she moved there. She was on her way to audition for the Minnesota Philharmonic, slipped on the ice, like you, and had a terrible sprain on her left hand. Even with her hurting hand, she taught at the MacPhail Center for Music for several years. Finally, her hand healed, and she's now working on her Master's in music performance at the Royal Danish Academy of Music in Copenhagen.

It just took her several years to recuperate. I can introduce you to her if you want to talk to her. Her story is, remarkably, a lot like yours."

"Thanks, Alex. I remember her when she was concertmaster in the Portland Youth Philharmonic when I was in the Young String Ensemble. She's exceptional, but I don't feel like talking to anyone. I just want to be left alone."

We talked for a spell longer, and they left.

Nita Van Pelt, the Lake Oswego High School orchestra conductor, and countless friends from the orchestra come to visit me—all simultaneously. They're all so earnest in their sympathy for me. They all chipped in to present me with an enormous bouquet. I thank them, but I just want all of them to leave me alone.

Nita says, "Theo, I know a girl, Julie DeLeo...."

I interrupt, "Thanks, Nita, but Alex already attempted to put me in touch with her."

"You're so lucky to have Alex as your violin teacher."

"I don't think I'll be needing her again for quite some time—if ever."

"Theo, don't lose hope. You never know what can happen. If you need anything, contact me."

They all left, finally.

Claire comes to visit.

"Theo, I miss you. I hope you're doing okay."

My feelings for Claire are mixed. I tell her, "I'm surviving but would rather just be alone."

"It's not good for you to be alone all the time. Do you want me to stay or leave?"

"I.... I don't know. I just want to be left alone."

A tear comes out of her eye. "I'll leave then."

I say nothing. With her shoulders slumped, she leaves. I feel horrible, but it's something I must do. She calls me countless times. After a while, I don't even answer her calls or texts. I don't want to talk to anyone. Anesthetized are all the romantic feelings I felt for her at the prom. I hurt her by my demeanor, but I don't like her or anyone else hounding me all the time.

Everyone is well-intentioned, but they become a giant albatross around my neck, just dripping with sympathy. Everyone expects me to do something, but I don't feel like doing anything. I need to get away from everyone and find my own path. I find myself sufficiently cold-hearted and rude to everyone—including Claire.

Perhaps Nita and Ben have some salient points. I need to figure out how not to lose hope and to get my stem and root to do U-turns.

9. Mount Tabor

I get a text from Ben, "Hey Theo, what are you doing now?"

"Nothing," I reply.

"You want to do something cool?"

"No, I don't want to do anything cool or see anyone. I just want to stay here and sulk in my bedroom."

"Sorry, kid," Ben replies. "Sit tight and wear some warm clothes."

About half an hour later, I hear a motorcycle pull up in front of our house. Ben gets off it, carrying an extra helmet. The doorbell rings. He hands me a helmet and points to a big bad looking motorcycle parked in the driveway.

"What? You're driving a motorcycle, a Harley Davidson no less?"

"Johnny Dove died and willed it to me."

"So, Johnny just died suddenly! He was a good guy, and he just died? How's Maxx taking it?"

"It's too early to tell. Many members of the church are consoling him now."

We walk up to the enormous machine.

"Her name is Honey," Ben says. "She got this name because she's the color of honey and purrs as smooth as honey when she's warmed up. Get on the back."

"What do I hold on to?"

"Me," Ben says.

I feel uncomfortable putting my arms around Dr. Dawson. Not only is this weird, but after we get going, I'm terrified. The beast below is not as sweet as honey; it's like a frothing and foaming mad bull.

"Just roll with the turns," Ben yells, "and try to enjoy the ride."

Honey sounds smoother. I'm feeling more confident. We drive across town and over the Ross Island Bridge to Mt. Tabor. The wind feels good, and I'm glad Ben forced me to go with him. We drive up to Mt. Tabor, wind around the road, and stop at a reservoir.

Ben says, "Mt. Tabor is an extinct volcano. This was my backyard when I grew up. I knew every nook and cranny of this place. There are several reservoirs here; they're currently used for Portland's drinking water. They're unsure what to do with them, as keeping them safe is hard."

"You want to know something really stupid that I did here when I was a kid?"

"Sure," I say.

"When I was in grade school, a friend and I discovered you could release the air out of tires with the backside of a tire valve cap. You need to insert it into the valve, turn it, and the air will come out of the tires. We came up here to this very spot and let air out of the tires of a few cars and thought it was great fun. When we returned to get our bikes, they were gone, and a Mount Tabor security guard was standing there next to the empty bike rack."

He said, "You want your bikes back; you get your mothers, bring them back here, and I'll give them to you. You let the air out of several car tires. Why in the hell did you do this?"

We both stood there wondering the same thing. We went to our homes, got our mothers, and suffered their wrath.

"Why did you do such a stupid thing?" I ask Ben.

"Theo, I did many stupid things when I was young for no good reason."

We drive as far as we can and then walk up to the top of the mountain. As we look down at the city, we can see one of the reservoirs.

Ben continues, "Years ago we could drive cars up here, but it became too crowded, and the cars destroyed the view and the ambiance. It was partly due to people like me."

"How's that?" I ask.

"It's a long story. I'll try to make it short. When I was in high school, I got a job in a grocery store as a 'box boy.' The only reason I got this job was so I could buy a car. I needed a car in high school like a hole in the head. I got the car only to take girls up here and make out with them overlooking the city when I should have been concentrating on schoolwork."

"Seriously?" I questioned.

"Do you want to know another stupid thing I did?"

"Sure."

"One evening when I was working at the grocery store, two guys walked into the store pointing guns at everyone, demanding money. I was in the back of the store in the meat department, where there was a phone on the wall. Instead of calling 911, I walked to the front to see what was happening. Two men with nylon stockings pulled over their heads were pointing guns at us. I was so stupid. I just wanted to see what was going on."

I ask, "What happened?"

"They successfully robbed the store, thanks to me not calling 911. Do you want to know another stupid thing I did?"

"Sure, this is fun."

For the first time since my hand injury, I didn't think about it.

"It happened again. I made the same stupid mistake. The same robbers came again and robbed the store."

"Did you not call 911 again?"

"Of course not; stupid teenagers never learn from their stupidity. Do you want to know an even stupider thing that I did?"

"There's more?"

"The phone rang, and it was a local news station. They asked me what had happened. I told them I was getting used to this, as this was the second armed robbery at this grocery store. The news station broadcasts my interview every hour on the hour all over Portland. I even told them my name. They recorded the call and didn't tell me they would use it on the radio."

"What happened next?" I ask.

"I got fired."

"Why'd they fire you?"

"The store was a big chain and didn't like having one of its 'box boys' normalize armed robbers at its stores."

"That sucks," I say.

"What can you learn, Theo, from my stupid youthful decisions?"

As Ben was attempting to teach me a lesson, I had to think about this, so I said, "I never realized how stupid you are."

10.   Homecoming Party

"Claire, you must go to the homecoming party with Fred," announces my mom.

"But I don't like Fred. I despise him."

"Oh, poppycock," my mom mocks. "It's not a big deal to have him pick you up and take you there. It's a big party, and all the popular boys and girls will be there. You're a star, and the kids there want to see you. Besides, most girls would give their eye-teeth to have Fred Freemark take them to the homecoming party!"

"Again. I despise Fred and don't want to go with him."

Later that day, my mom hands me the phone. She's talking to Fred's mother, and they decide I need to speak to Fred.

Fred's on the line, he says. "Come on, Claire, let me take you to the homecoming party. All of my friends will be there."

"I don't think so," I say.

"Great. I'll pick you up at six on Friday."

"No. I don't want to go to the party with you." I hang up the phone.

I'm ready on the day of the party, expecting my mom to take me. I hear a strange-sounding horn in our driveway.

"Surprise." Mom says, "Fred's out there. Aren't you going to get in his car?"

"No," I say. "I told Fred I don't want to go with him."

"Sometimes, you must bend the rules to move up in our world," Mom replies.

"Where else should I bend the rules, mom? If I get in his car, should I bend the rules when he tries to kiss me? How far should I let him go?"

"Claire, you're acting like a petulant child. You'll insult him if you don't get into his car. Besides, you need to date boys like Fred Freemark."

"Why?" I ask.

"Because his family and ours are of the same class."

I feel like giving my mom the finger. After several honks, he gets out of his car and knocks on the door.

He looks irritated. "Why didn't you come when I honked?"

"I told you I don't want to go to the party with you."

"Was my horn not loud enough?"

"Fred, are you listening to me? I don't want to go to the party with you."

"Are you serious? I thought you were joking."

"I've never been more serious about anything in my life."

My mom strolls into the room. "Hi, Fred. I hope you two have fun at the homecoming party."

"I'm not going with Fred. I'm not a well-trained dog that comes running with a wagging tail at the sound of a weird-sounding horn. Please leave Fred!"

"You can't talk to me this way. Everybody respects me."

"Well, I don't respect you at all. Again, please leave—now!" I yell. Fred walks away in a huff.

My mom snarls, "I can't believe how you treated him."

"I can't believe you arranged for this to happen. If you don't take me, I'm not going."

"You must attend this party, as many of your fans will be there. I'm mortified at how you treated Fred."

"Mom, by trying to force him on me it should mortify you."

"I'm not sure what the Freemarks will think of this, young lady."

"I could not care less what they think."

My mom drives me to the party, and neither of us says a word.

I walk into this traditional homecoming party alone—it makes me feel empowered. The football team won the state championship this year. Everyone thinks it's because of Fred Freemark—the football team captain. The rally squad girls are jumping up and down, waving their pom-poms in tight, colorful little outfits, and putting on a show to support their victory. Fred's gloating, and everyone has their eyes on him. The school principal gives a speech praising the football team's victory and presents Fred with a huge ostentatious-looking trophy. Then a rock band plays loud and out-of-tune garbage. Everyone dances and parties. Fred's talking to three guys who I don't recognize from our school; they look like super-spoiled rich kids—like Fred.

The atmosphere of this event is so bad; I can't stand it. I take a break and walk behind the school to escape it all. I sit in the bleachers looking at the stupid football field. It's quieter out here, but I can still hear the awful music in the background. I can hear a few lonely birds chirping too. Fred's three friends must have followed me; they all sit behind me. They pretend to be carrying on an innocent conversation.

One of them asks, "Do you like beer?"

Another says, "I like beer."

The third one says, "Who doesn't like beer? Hey girl, do you like beer?"

I get up, but one pushes me down on the shoulder. Another one plays with my hair. I can't get away from them!

"She's a feisty girl," one of them says.

"Hey Claire, Fred says you're a hot one. Devil's Triangle, here we come."

I see Jay Fowler, one of Fred's football buddies, and several other football players walk toward us.

"What's going on?" Jay asks.

"Nothin," says one, "just a little devil's-tri stuff."

Jay's a linebacker. He looks like he weighs about two hundred pounds. Jay and his friends don't look so happy about my situation.

Jay asks, "What's devil's-tri stuff?"

One of them says, "Oh, just some fun stuff, that's all."

Jay says two words to them, "Back off."

"Who do you think you are, getting in the way of our fun?"

"Your worst nightmare," Jay says.

They look at Jay and the other linebackers with him and sheepishly slink away.

"Are you okay?" Jay asks.

'No. I'm scared shitless. Those creeps were up to something."

Jay says, "When I saw them follow you out, I knew in my bones something was up, so I asked these guys to come with me."

We walk back to the party together and walk up to Fred.

Jay says, "Fred, your three friends were trying to mess with Claire."

Fred replies, "You mean Donald, Gym, and Brett? They're harmless. I've known them for a long time. Their parents and mine hang out together at the Exclusive River Country Club. I invited them to the party."

"Harmless my ass," I retort. "Is the Devil's Triangle a harmless thing? Is grabbing my arm and not letting go harmless?"

I'm fuming mad.

"Oh, they were just having a little fun," Fred says.

I tell Fred, "You're a genuine piece of work; all the rumors I hear about you are true."

I knew this comment would drive Fred nuts. So, rather than telling a specific lie, as he did about me with Donald, Brett, and Gym, I thought it would be more painful for him to wonder about what people were saying about him.

I walk out of the party. Jay and his girlfriend, Ann, follow me out.

"Would you like us to take you home?" Jay asks.

"That would be nice," I say. "Do you mind, Ann?"

"I'd love an opportunity to leave this dreadful party," Ann replies.

On the way home, Jay says to me, "Fred's an asshole."

"I thought you and his other football buddies worshiped him?"

"Not me," Jay says.

"Me neither," Ann says. "Finally, we can get away from Fred's big victory party. I hate him."

Jay adds, "I know too much about him. I had to 'play ball,' so to speak, to help win the pennant for our school. Since football season is over, I feel liberated to be away from him. Stay away from him; he's toxic and evil."

"Amen," Ann affirms.

Jay says, "I need to tell you something about him, but now's not the right time. Do you mind giving me your phone number? I'll call you later. But first, I have to process what I know."

I text Jay my phone number. He and Ann walk with me to the door.

"Stay safe," Jay says. "Be careful, and above all, stay away from Fred!"

"Amen," Ann repeats.

11. Ugly Room Ugly Job

I need to get away from everyone. I have about a thousand dollars in savings, which would help me find a place to live. Some old apartments are across the street from the College of Naturopathic Medicine at the end of the Ross Island bridge; one is right next to a highway. They're asking three hundred dollars a month for a single room. There's a sink in there and enough room for a bed. I have a sleeping bag and an air mattress—this is it. Four rooms share one bathroom. You can hear and smell traffic twenty-four seven with the highway next to the window. The old guy in the next room coughs like his lungs are on fire all day and night. He smokes like a chimney. I can smell the smoke—like a bad dream that never goes away. I figure this is better than everybody bothering me all day, trying to cheer me up. As Ben suggested, I need space to figure out how to get my stem and root to do U-turns.

If I don't find a job, my thousand dollars will evaporate quickly. I take walks to think and pick up bottles and cans. Thanks to the Oregon Bottle Bill, I can get ten cents apiece for them, which buys me a hamburger now and then. I walk by a McDanny's restaurant near Portland State University with a help-wanted sign in the window. I go in and fill out a job application. The manager looks at my application, studies it, and looks me up and down—as if it's a college application.

He finally says, "Theo Hall, my name is Harold Sweeny. Why do you want to work at McDanny's?"

I wondered if there was some political answer he needed to hear, like, "Because I want to be a part of the McDanny's culture and someday aspire to be like you," or I could answer with, "because I need a job, you stupid idiot."

Instead, I politely say, "I'm in transition and would like to work for a well-known company with which I can be proud to be affiliated."

He seems to like my answer and hires me. My first job is to watch some training videos.

"You can watch the videos today or tomorrow and report for duty the following day. Doing it the McDanny's way requires a well-trained staff."

He looks at me while uttering McDanny's name in a reverential way. I look at him and act like we're two football fans praising the same team.

I watch training videos for two days. McDanny's has hamburgers, fish and chicken sandwiches, breakfast items, and every other product down to the science of taste and profit with little or no nutrition. Their french fries come frozen, made in a factory that extracts everything from them, adds artificial flavor, and partially cooks them; then they're dropped into the deep fry vat where they get golden brown in cheap processed oil.

"To make french fries," Harold instructs, "after coming out of the deep fry vat, you salt them with this specially designed shaker; then you put them into the bag or box with this tool."

He shows how the gadget scoops up the fries. He shakes them expertly while snuggling them into a large box or a small bag. The 30-year-old manager extols this unique knowledge to me with the experience of 15 years at McDanny's, working here since high school—half of his life.

I enthusiastically concur, "That's exactly how the training videos explained how to do it."

"So," says the proud manager, "We'll start you with fries. You will make them, the McDanny's way. You will bag them, the McDanny's way, and we'll pay you with the money you make for us by doing it the McDanny's way."

I was lucky because my left hand, which holds the violin, was the one that was damaged. My right hand, which holds the bow, holds the scoop. I can hold the bag or the box with no pain with my left hand because I don't have to arch my wrist to reach the strings with my fingers.

"Now remember, don't make too many fries, or they won't be fresh. Only make enough fries as orders are coming in. If the store is empty, don't make any fries. If many people are in line, make more fries so our valued customers won't have to wait. It's a delicate balance. We don't want to serve bad fries, and we don't want to throw old fries out. If you don't do it right, we're in big trouble. We must make at least a twenty-three percent overall profit at this franchise, although fries make a ninety percent profit. When I started working at this store, our profit margin was twenty-one percent. I've increased it by two percent!"

He's so proud of himself; I wonder if this is all there is to him. All this is so boring to me I can hardly stand it. I feel sorry for this poor dude who started here 15 years ago and is still here, proudly making a 23% profit for the franchise owner.

From what I remember from the training videos, it would be fun to impress the manager, so I say to him, "Yields are important. We calculate a yield for the ounces of fries per bag and box to ensure our employees are not cheating our customers with too few fries or over-stuffing and mashing the fries into the bag or box, which destroys our yields. The shake and sundae yields tell us about the condition of our pump check valves and whether they're beating enough air into the mix to make it light and tasty while telling us whether we'll make money on it. If it's too heavy, it's not only un-refreshing but destroys our yield. If we're going through too many cans of magic sauce per Big Mick, more than likely, our employee is clicking the gun too many times, or there's something wrong with the magic sauce gun. We must check all the equipment for proper operation continually. We also must ensure that our employees do everything the McDanny's way, as clearly spelled out in our excellent training videos. After all, if we don't make a profit for the franchise owner, we shouldn't work here."

"That's impressive, Theo. You should consider management training. Let's see how you do on the floor, and we can go from there."

The next day, I worked at the fry station for eight hours. I got a break to eat a free double cheeseburger with fries. This is the most boring thing I have ever done, but I need the money to pay for my lousy room with the traffic and the coughing guy in the next room. After French fries, I learned grillwork, assembly, and counterwork.

The soft-serve ice cream machine stops working one revolting day when I'm at the counter. The ice cream won't come out. I was exceptionally good at all the mechanical devices in the restaurant. I must stop the machine, open it up from the front and scrape the stuck mixture from the sides of the stainless-steel mixing chamber. The night crew, who cleaned the device, put it back together incorrectly, so it jammed.

With my humiliating McDanny's apron on, trying to fix the machine, who other than Fred Freemark, with some new football buddies, walks into the restaurant. Emblazoned on their football jerseys are the Portland State Vikings.

I think, "I guess Fred's grades weren't good enough to get him into Yale, even with all of his father's money and influence."

"So, the late great nationally known fiddle player makes it to the big time," Fred laughs.

He sees me attempting to fix the machine, saying, "I'd like a soft-serve ice cream cone."

"Sorry, Fred, the machine isn't working correctly, and there will be no soft serve ice cream for at least a half-hour."

"But I want some now. Let me speak to the manager."

All of Fred's friends laugh. Fred is making such a big scene that Harold Sweeney, the highly experienced manager, emerges from the back of the kitchen.

"Is there a problem here?" he asks.

"Yes," says Fred. "This crew boy spoke to me in a derogatory manner. I asked for soft-serve ice cream, and Crew Boy told me to 'fuck off.'"

"Did you say this?" demands Harold.

"No," I answered.

"Apologize to our valued customer," he ordered.

"I did nothing wrong. I didn't say what he's accusing me of. Why should I apologize for something I didn't say?"

Harold Sweeny says to Fred, "We apologize for any misunderstandings here. Is there anything we can do to make things right?"

By now, the ice cream machine is doing its job.

"I'd like a free ice cream cone and an apology from Crew Boy for telling me to fuck off, or I'll sue McDanny's for an employee insulting a paying customer. My father is wealthy."

"How about we give free ice cream cones to all your friends too," the frightened manager states.

All four of Fred's friends enthusiastically agree. I have to make five ice cream cones for Fred and his friends. I make Fred's ice cream cone smaller than the others hoping for a humiliating response. Sure enough, he grabs the bait.

"Hey, mine is smaller than the others."

I say nothing and try to hide my smile. His friends snicker behind his back.

My manager who didn't see my subtle attempt at humor says, "Now, apologize to our valued customer for swearing at him in a derogatory manner."

"I will not apologize for something I didn't do."

"Have it your way," says the manager, who probably said, "Have it your way" countless times to customers who don't want pickles on their hamburgers. He'll charge them for the extra pickle if they want over two standard pickles, so his yields won't go down.

After Fred and his friends leave, the manager calls me into the back room.

"Theo," he explains with fifteen years of McDanny's experience, having increased the profit margin at this franchise by two percent, "You can't talk to our customers this way. You may know a lot about internal operations, how to profit from watching our training videos and learning from me, but you can't make a profit if you swear at our valued customers."

"I didn't swear at him. He made that up."

"I'm going to put you back on french fries for now. You will not be at the counter until I feel you can be nicer to our guests."

"But Harold, I did nothing wrong. I didn't tell Fred to fuck off. That was a lie."

"The customer is always right," he fumed. "Now get back to the French fry station and do your fucking job!"

"I have a better idea," I say. I take off the McDanny's apron, throw it on the floor, and say, "I quit."

As I walk out of the store, the manager bellows, "The price of five ice cream cones will come out of your last paycheck!"

I turn to Harold and say, "Look, Harold, you're so brainwashed that your life is meaningless. You make a profit for the franchise owner so he can water ski on Lake Oswego. You're a corporate slave and don't even know it."

"At least I have a job with benefits," is his reply, "and you don't."

He was right; I would soon discover.

12. Self-Defense Class

A month after the incident at the homecoming party, I determine I need to know how to protect myself. Ben told us about Belle Brown, his self-defense instructor, who teaches at the Portland Police Training Facility. I discovered she teaches classes for women there too.

I call the training facility, "I'd like to speak to Belle Brown."

"Please hold."

"This is Belle Brown; how can I help you?"

"My name is Claire Devine. Recently I had a close call. I feel so vulnerable that I must know how to defend myself if this happens again."

"Were you hurt?"

"Not physically."

"You can explain the details later. You've come to the right place. The next session starts in a week. Would you like to sign up?"

"Absolutely."

"Sign up at the link that I'll send you, and we'll see you at the Portland Police Training Facility next week. How'd you hear about our program?"

"I didn't hear about a specific program; I heard about you from Dr. Ben Dawson. He's a friend."

"Ah hah, Ben's one of my favorite students. He's outstandin' as a fighter and ironically as a pastor. I've been thinking of attending his church but haven't had the time. He's an advocate for women's rights. He's adorable too. I wish he was single."

"He's cute alright, especially in his cargo pants," I laugh.

"Don't laugh about his cargo pants. I want you to get a pair for yourself and wear them to the lessons."

"Are you serious?"

"You'll see," Belle says. "See you next week."

I have to lie to my mother about using her BMW. I feel so stupid in her flashy car, but it would have taken two hours to get to the Portland Police Training Facility on the bus with transfers. I tell her I want to go shopping for some clothes at Washington Square; this is an acceptable use of her car instead of learning how to defend myself against Fred's friends. I go to Target and buy a pair of cargo pants for women instead of buying cutesy clothes at Nordstrom. I'll just tell mom I couldn't find anything that I like.

A five-foot-three athletic-looking black lady enters the room. "Hi, my name is Belle Brown. I'll be teachin' you how to survive an assault. If anyone is successful at attemptin' to assault you, they'll be sorry they ever got near you. I'll show you techniques that'll save your life. Listen carefully and remember, practice makes perfect. We need to practice the moves repeatedly until they become second nature."

We learned several moves to counter situations like I was in at the homecoming party. When Brett, Donald, or Gym touched my hair, I should have run as fast as possible to get away and not allow them to push me down on my shoulder and grab my arm. According to Belle, running away is the best form of defense. But it was too late when they held my arm down, and I couldn't run away. Instead, I'm taught to pull the guy toward me and strike him with my elbow in the face, abdomen, or crotch as hard as possible. If the attacker faces me, I'm taught to kick him with my legs in the same places. Legs are much more powerful than arms. I practice kicking high into the air to hit faces—like a Radio City Music Hall Rockette. Over several months, we practiced this move repeatedly, to where my legs are becoming powerful self-defense tools. Belle is also fond of plucking, using your hand as a hook to pull the attacker down wherever you can. I could have plucked the arm off my shoulder, perhaps kicked him, and run away.

After class one day, she told me that Ben enjoys plucking. She said he used it in a parking lot against two guys who tried to mess with him.

"They didn't have a chance," she said. "Pluckin' his attacker's arm down gave him the chance to disable the three-hundred-pound beast. He turned around and kicked him in the abdomen which disabled him. This gave him the perfect opportunity to put the other guy out of business. They were both severely injured in the end."

"Ben did this?"

"I could go into more detail, but you'd better ask Ben about it."

"This I will do."

I admire Ben more and more each day.

As the classes advance, Belle pulls out something that looks like handheld steel spikes.

"This is a tiger claw. It's one of your best weapons. We'll practice with this until you become a fierce Tiger Lady."

There's a dummy that we use as a would-be assailant. Belle will push this guy toward us rather forcefully. We're taught to kick it as hard as we can with our leg, then use our tiger claw anywhere we can. I enjoy hearing the satisfying thud when I get a solid kick in his crotch. With the tiger claw, I especially like to aim for the eyes. Any man attempting to mess with me again will lose his eyesight. I yell like a mad tigress with glee whenever I get a solid hit in the eyes. I love my tiger claw. It makes me feel safe and empowered.

"You're a fierce animal," Belle keeps telling me over and over until it's ingrained in my mind.

After months of training, I can disable the target every time. Belle has to get a new dummy, as I've destroyed one of them. I derive great satisfaction from doing this. Some of the other girls are here because they want to get school credit. They don't realize the importance of defending themselves—I do. The Bretts, Donalds, and Gyms of the world will get what's coming to them if they ever attempt to mess with this Tiger Lady again.

"Claire," Belle says, "Keep your tiger claw with you. If you ever go on a walk at night, alone, or to a dark place, wear your cargo pants, and keep it in one of the buttoned-down pockets. When you're dressed up, the next place for it is in your hand. Always carry it in your purse. Never leave home without it."

I bow and say, "Yes, Obi-Wan Kenobi. I will comply and tell all my friends about your wisdom and strength of mind and body."

"Claire, here's a fact to think about: One in five women in the United States experience completed or attempted rape during their lifetime. You're not alone. Don't be weak. Run away as fast as you can or fight back!"

I open my mouth wide and growl like an angry tiger.

13. Tent City

Someone finds out where I live. There's a sign on my door that reads, "Fiddlehead Flophouse." Soon after this incident, there are countless knocks on my door from perhaps well-meaning and not-so-well-meaning people who found my address from the social grapevine.

I'm tired of people hounding me to get my act together or ridiculing me, so I move out of this room with my sleeping bag and air mattress. How can I ever make a U-Turn if everyone tells me what to do with my life? I find an old, abandoned canvas tent near the railroad tracks near a weird store called Cargo; it sells restored Asian antiques that people, like Claire's mother, want to display in their homes. Since I don't have an address, no one can bother me here. There are so many places in Portland to get free food for the homeless that I'm not starving. I still pick up cans and bottles to buy toothpaste and other things. Finally, no one knows where I am. I can sit here all day in peace.

It's cold down here. I walk a block to a clothing store for homeless people. I find a hoodie with fancy-looking hand-embroidered lettering on the back. It reads, Peace Through Global Domination. The tag on the inside says, Jackson, Taylor, Olongapo City, Philippines. I need to ask my birth father about this because he has been in and out of the naval base at Subic Bay countless times as a naval officer. My father says Olongapo City is just a short walk from the naval base across from the aptly named Shit River. The river got its name because it smells like raw sewage.

I take a walk around my new neighborhood. A couple is sitting on the sidewalk together. They look blitzed out on drugs. The white girl looks to be about twenty. The black guy who is with her looks to be the same age.

The girl says, "Welcome to the neighborhood. Looks like you got that tent—fuckin'."

I point to my tent. "Yeh, that's the one I'm in."

"Stay away from the fucker in the tent next to yours."

"Why?"

"Name's Dick Wolf. Bad dude. You do blues?"

"What are blues?"

"They fuckin' make you feel good."

I feel sorry for both of them. They look pathetic. They're both strung out on something and sit there like stoned zombies.

"Why do you do pills?"

"Started doing pills. My mother kicked me out. I fucked up. At four o'clock in the morning, I left. I do pills."

"When did you start doing pills?"

"I started pills when I was seventeen. Got sick—fuckin'. I got clean for a few days. I got a job and fuckin'. My parents didn't want to talk to me. I stay out here with him."

She points to the guy sitting next to her. "My birthday was January third."

"How'd you get into pills?"

The guy has been staring at the street the whole time; he finally looks up and says, "I was with my brother; I got kicked out. Ever since I started doin' blues, I never stopped."

The girl speaks again, "We had children; then he got clean; then we got hotel. I'd sneak out and see him. He fuckin', he knew I couldn't be out here. I went to the hotel to bring him food, so the cleaning lady opened the door, and he was out on the bed all fucked up. Fuckin' pills everywhere on his face, he od'd. Traumatized the fuck out of me. I tried his pills. I just started buyin' em—fuckin'. So we just started doing em together. He od'd in the hotel—fuckin."

The guy seems to pay attention now. He says, "I thought I was sleepin'. Woke up with firefighters—family all around. I stopped for two days."

"What do you do for money?"

"I don't panhandle. I sell legal stuff for money."

"Like what?"

"Coke, Pepsi, newspapers."

The girl chimes in, "I sit here every day. My mother gives me money while I'm out here. Every time I talk to my mom, she asks when I'll get clean. I don't call them anymore. If I do, she'll come out here and bring something to eat—fuckin."

Someone walks by saying, "Hey man, I got a job."

She yells back, "Fuckin'."

I can't make much sense out of what they're saying, but one thing is sure, they're stoned out of their fuckin' minds.

I walk around my new neighborhood in search of a place to eat. I have enough money to last for a while, but I have some extra free cash if I pick up some extra bottles or cans. While searching for cans, I encounter a young woman sitting on an overturned shopping cart.

She sees me, takes a big drag on her cigarette, and says, "Dude, you're cute. Do you date?"

Big hoop earrings dance on her shoulders as she talks.

"Date? Do I look like I need a date?"

"Date. You know what I mean. Quick time fifty bucks. Longer time in a car, one hundred twenty. A hotel one fifty. If you buy me food in hotel, one hundred."

I finally get the picture; date means time with a prostitute in Tent City.

"How old are you?"

"Twenty-Three."

She has long, stringy hair.

"How long have you been living here?"

"Since I was eighteen."

"Do you feel safe down here?"

"There're a lota guys rapin' females."

"Where are you from?"

"Puerto Rico."

"What's your name?"

"Jane."

"How'd you get down here, Jane?"

"Childhood, I felt neglected. I got my ass whooped a lot. When I was 14, I got involved with an 18-year-old. One day he got killed in front of me. People stopped talkin' to me. Ran into this guy who was hustlin'."

She lights up another cigarette from the last one.

Since I finally realize that most homeless people are on drugs, I ask her, "Do you do drugs?"

"He was using Fentanyl. Ever since then, I keep going on and on with it. I had no money. I started doin' dates for drugs."

Now that I'm schooled on what a "date" is on the streets, I understand what she's telling me.

"Seen people shoot up. I was curious enough puttin' a needle in my arm. Every day I be lookin' for dates. I'd rather have a bag than eat."

"Have you tried rehab?"

"Went to rehab—relapsed. Date drags me into his car. Starts beatin' on me; takes my purse and cell phone."

"How could people be so cruel?" I ask.

"I'm twenty-three. I don't deserve this; I need to get my shit together."

"Do you have contact with your family?"

"I don't contact my family. I lost myself. I'm willing to give myself one more shot. I'm lost, lonely, and confused. I don't need to get punched in the face. I just need to get a fix and eat something. Pills are not cool. Don't take any type of pill. Look at me now. You fuck up your life."

"What's your living status now?"

"I jump from friends to friends' houses. Shelters. Purse stolen. I have no ID. I've lost everything because of my addiction. House, family, respect. Toughest thing now is how to keep these demons away from me."

She lights up another cigarette. I feel so sorry for this woman—what a waste. Drugs make money, and the people making them and selling them on the street don't care about human life. I realize I was raised in a bubble. My new neighbors result from human greed.

When I walk by the Portland Rescue Mission, I can't help but wander in out of curiosity. They have a stack of booklets called Street Roots Rose City Resource. It lists all the places for homeless people to find food, clothing, or shelter. I take several copies with me. I stuff them in my cargo pants. Ben's obsession with cargo pants is making more and more sense each day.

14. She Was Just Seventeen

I see her standing there, on the street meridian, skinny, cold, and afraid, with a cardboard sign that reads, "Hungry, cold, need help." She looks so vulnerable I can hardly stand it. I see a pickup truck pull up next to her with a Confederate flag flying and an empty gun rack in the back window; it skids to a stop at a green light. A beefy white guy with a bald head gets out of the truck's passenger side and starts toward the girl. She runs away so fast he can't keep up with her. The guys in the truck give up and take off, squealing their tires with black diesel smoke billowing from the exhaust pipes. The image of this poor thing haunts me. I see her walking around my neighborhood and follow her. I feel like a stalker. She sneaks into a tent hidden from the street view. I feel sorry for the girl. When she's gone from the tent, I bring some canned tuna, water, and other canned food items that don't need a can opener. I also include apples, celery, and other fresh things. Since I started this, I don't see her begging for money on the street meridian. I guess all she needs is food. It's a stretch providing the food, but it gives me great satisfaction to know she isn't begging for food. She's not in her tent when it's not zipped tightly. She leaves it slightly open when gone but tightly zipped when in the tent. I bring her food regularly. I also leave a copy of Street Roots.

The freight train blasts through the neighborhood several times a day. It creeps along the tracks between brick buildings; the horn is so loud that rats scurry away from it. The notes on the horn are a low D sharp, middle F sharp, G sharp, B, and an octave higher D. It's a B Major 6th chord. On the one hand, it's a catchy major chord; on the other hand, it drives me insane because from years of use, some of the train horns are out of tune, and it's so loud that it makes my brain boil. It's a daily reminder that certain things plow through your life unwanted, like disease, hunger, loneliness, inhumanity, poverty, death, drug addiction, and ironically,

Tchaikovsky's Violin Concerto in D. If only a symphony could create such a magnificently intrusive sound at the beginning or end of a composition. Perhaps Philip Glass could pull it off. Just a blast, throughout the piece, with no chord changes, until relief comes with a change of key, but the same blast. As the train passes by, the doppler effect changes the horn's pitch, and I can hear the train in the distance slowly plowing its way through Portland's Eastside. An orchestra could achieve the doppler effect with a glissando, one-half step lower during the blast.

I find a music store in the neighborhood and buy some blank musical staff paper. The first note of my piece is a B Major 6th chord like the train horn. At first, I score it for a quintet, but upon reflection, I need to score it for a full orchestra to get the full effect of the repulsively pestilent horn. I may even have one note slightly out of tune for the most realistic effect.

As I enjoy peaceful anonymity with notes flying onto staff paper, I hear a car stop and turn off the engine. I poke my head out of the opening, and a black Cadillac SUV just parked there. A guy in a suit, driving the car, opens the window.

Dammit, they found me. Then the back window of the SUV opens, and Miss Seventeen is sitting in the back seat. I can hardly recognize her, as she looks like a well-cared-for, pretty, high-school girl.

The guy asks Miss Seventeen, "Honey, is this the guy?"

I think that my goose is cooked as they could accuse me of stalking. She responds, "Yes, daddy, he's the one."

I feel like running.

The guy in the suit gets out of the SUV and says, "Son, you saved my daughter's life."

"Why do you say that?" I ask.

Miss Seventeen gets out of the car, comes to me, and hugs me. "I followed you after seeing you deliver food and water to my tent."

Her hair smells like fragrant roses blowing in a soft breeze—unlike my smelly canvas tent.

"What's your name?" she asks.

"Bob," I don't want anyone to know my first name, as it's all over the news that Theo Hall, a violin prodigy, is missing.

"I'm Claudia." she smiles.

I ask her, "How'd you end up in a tent—like me?"

"It's a long story. I'll make it short. My mother took custody of me when my parents got divorced. My father had to leave the country on a business trip. Without going into detail, things got terrible with my mom. I had to get out of the house and ended up down here. When my father returned to Portland, I told him where I live. He came immediately and brought me home."

Her father wept. "Bob, as a token of my gratitude for saving my daughter's life, here's something to help you out." He hands me an envelope.

"My business card is in there. If you ever need anything at all just call me. If you do to others what you did for my daughter, I thank you sincerely, as Claudia means the world to me."

As they drive away, Claudia pokes her head out the window, blows me a kiss, and smiles. I'm in shock. A stack of $100 bills is in my tent. I now have $5,000 in cash to fit into my buttoned-down cargo pants pocket. The business card reads, Brevard Hallstrom, CEO, Hallstrom Properties. Commercial Real Estate Developers Worldwide.

15. He Was Just Seventy-Five

Lying on the sidewalk, shaking, he looks up at me. He can hardly lift his head. He's coughing, shivering, and ignored by passersby. His teeth are rotting out. He has several layers of clothing on with a space blanket covering him. He rests his head on a pile of old newspapers. Across the street is a small cafe. I go in and ask for a cup of soup to go. The cashier looks at me skeptically. I point out the window to the older black man lying on the sidewalk. Immediately there's a knowing look on the cashier's face.

She pulls out a paper cup from under the counter, fills it with hot soup, and nods to me knowingly. "No charge," she says.

I walk over to the poor man, lift his head, and offer him some soup. The look on his face is unreal. He sips the soup gently, as he's so weak that he can hardly move. I sit with him for about a half-hour as he can barely get the soup down. I don't know what else to do. The old guy is in this spot every day. I always get him some soup from the cafe across the street.

After getting to know him, he says to me, "We killed so many innocent people in Vietnam. We'd throw hand grenades into their hooches made of straw. We blew up entire families. They ordered me to do it. We're taught to call Vietnamese villagers "Gooks" in boot camp. The dummies we used as target practice were short, with straw hats. I can't live with myself no more. I'm better off dead."

"What's your name?" I ask.

"Henry Doyle."

I point to myself, "Bob."

"Thanks for the soup, Bob."

He can hardly get the words out as he's old and feeble. People walk by me every day when I give him some soup. Even if I ask for some help, they ignore me.

"You're an angel of mercy, Bob."

He closes his eyes and falls asleep. Whenever the cashier in the cafe sees me, she knows what I want and gives me free soup.

While filling his cup, one cold and cloudy day, she says to me, "Now and then that poor guy leaves, but always comes back. He must go to the toilet somewhere. Thanks for helping him. I can't stand to see him there. I can hardly sleep at night knowing he's there."

"Me neither," I lament.

On another cold and clammy day, I shake him when I come to his spot with his soup. He doesn't move. People are just walking by, unconcerned; even when I ask for help, they ignore me. I feel for a pulse in his neck—nothing. I rush into the soup kitchen and tell the cashier to call 911 for an ambulance. About five minutes later, an ambulance shows up. The paramedics also feel for a pulse. They must feel something as they do CPR on him for an interminable time. Finally, they put an oxygen mask on him and put him in the back of the ambulance.

Before they close the back doors, I run to the ambulance and ask them where they'll take him. "We're headed to the VA ER on Pill Hill."

"Where's Pill Hill?"

The man points up to the West Hills. "Up there where the VA hospital is located. You can take the tram up there."

"How do you know he's a veteran?"

"Because the only thing on him are his dog tags."

The back door of the ambulance slams shut, and they take off with the siren blaring.

A week later, I walk to the Oregon Health and Science University medical center, partly at the base of the Willamette River. This is where the giant sculpture of red balloons sits. Alex and Ben told me the story of how they met here. Ben slammed into a lamppost, distracted by, "The most beautiful girl I had ever seen tying her shoe." The rest is history. They fell for each other.

I get on the tram and take it to the OHSU Medical Center on top of the famous Pill Hill. The covered pedestrian bridge leading to the VA Medical Center has a fantastic view. I take the elevators to the reception desk. I ask where Henry Doyle is, and they direct me to his room. When I get there, he's lying in a hospital bed. Two other veterans are lying in hospital beds in the room as well. A chaplain is walking out of his room.

Before entering, I stop the chaplain and ask him about Henry. "He's sleeping now," he says. "You should come back later today when he's awake."

"Is he okay?"

"How do you know him?" the chaplain asks.

"I found him on the street and gave him soup every day for several weeks. I had the ambulance come when he didn't respond to me."

"So, you're Bob, the kid he keeps talking about. Even in his sleep, he says that 'Bob is an angel of mercy.'"

"I don't know about that. I just gave him some hot soup."

"That's not what he says. He says that when he had no hope and was ready to die, you came along and 'gave a shit.' He claims you were the bridge between life and death for him."

"Hope?" I think to myself. Nita told me not to lose hope.

"So, what's the deal with him?" I ask.

"Since you're the only person who 'gives a shit' about him, I'll give you a window into his soul."

We're standing in the hall, so the chaplain leads me to an empty waiting room.

"Henry Doyle is a Vietnam Vet. They drafted him and ordered him into the jungles of Vietnam after just sixteen weeks of training. They taught this eighteen-year-old kid to kill, and he did so with patriotic zeal. His government told him to do unspeakable things. He's now suffering from what we call 'moral injury.' He can't live with himself because his moral upbringing differed from what the government taught and ordered him to do. On top of this, the suffering and death he saw and endured lives with him as Post-Traumatic Stress Disorder. Many of our Veterans suffer from both Moral Injury and Post-Traumatic Stress Disorder. Sadly, Mr. Doyle couldn't handle them both and ended up, like too many veterans, on the street."

"Is there any hope?" I ask.

"It takes a long time, but we have the resources at the VA to help him. I thank you for what you have done. Please come and visit him when you can, as you will probably be the only visitor he has outside of VA medical staff. According to his doctor, he's not doing well; he may not live much longer. Please come back soon."

I didn't know what to say or think. Me, an angel? No way. I'm a self-centered, privileged white kid. All I did was give the poor, suffering guy some soup.

"I have to go." I walk out.

The chaplain says, "Wait."

I stop.

"Thank you for caring."

I nod my head and walk on out.

16. He Was as Old as Doit

I take the tram down from the medical center. I sit on one of the few benches. A short old guy with an enormous nose using a cane takes his time getting on. I get up and give him my seat.

"What are you here for?" I ask.

"Canca," he mutters.

"What's your name?" I ask.

"Johnny."

"Yous?"

"Theo." I can't believe I blurted out my real name.

"You don't sound like you're from Portland," I say. "Where are you from?"

"Brooklyn, New Yoak," he answers.

"What brings you to Portland?"

"Da waah. They stationed me at Faat Lewis in Washington."

"What war?" I ask.

"I'm as old as doit, kid. Da Kowean Waah."

"What made you stay in Portland?" I ask.

"A goil."

"A what?" I ask again.

"A goil," he again replies.

"Oh, do you mean a girl?"

"Hell yes, kid. Wuddaya tink I said?"

"Sorry, your Brooklyn accent threw me off."

"I ain't got no accent. You da one wit da accent."

I laugh.

"Is the girl still around?" I ask.

"Na. She died several yeas ago; God rest huuh soul. When I married huuh, she had a kid."

When the tram lands at the bottom, we get off. He's struggling with his cane, so I help him.

"Hey kid," he says, "You look like you need a cup of coffee. Let me buy ya one."

"How about I buy you one?" I ask.

"It's on me, kid. I tink I got mooa money dan you do."

I look at my disheveled clothes. I'm looking homeless. We walk past the red balloon sculpture where Ben brags Alex proposed to him. We rest on the park bench   that looks at the balloon sculpture.

"Dis is a famous bench," Johnny says.

"How so?" I ask.

"Rememba, when I said dat da love of my life had a kid?"

"Yes."

"Dat kid is a smaat little fucka. He got famous. His even smaata goilfriend asked him to marry him right on dis bench we a sittin on."

My mouth drops open as I realize that Johnny Accardo is Ben's stepfather.

Another old guy walks by before I respond. "Johnny? Johnny Accardo? What the hell are you doing here? You're a sight for sore eyes. I miss your nightclubs so much. Portland will never be the same without them. It's all crappy stuff now. You had class. We could go into one of them, have dinner, dance to a group playing all the old standards, and you'd usually come around and greet us. You'd always remember my name."

"I rememba ya, Richaad. Ya always had a good-lookin' broad wit you."

"Ah those were my good old single days. One hooked me, and I was married to her for forty-five years. We went to your nightclubs until they shut down. She just died a few years ago. It's shitty lonely now."

"Wheadoya live?" Johnny asks.

"Tigard," the guy replies.

"Go see my stepson at da Lake Oswego Pragressive Choich. He'll help you out—gaunteed. Tell him I sent ya."

A crowd of older adults gather around us. Johnny Accardo knew a few people.

"Excuse me, "Johnny says. "I promised dis kid I'd get him a cup of coffee."

He bids them a farewell. We walk to the coffee shop.

"Whaddaya want?" he asks.

"Plain old coffee," I respond.

"Two plain old coffees," he tells the barista.

We sit down.

"I have something to tell you; Ben Dawson is my pastor, and his wife, Alexandria Savich is my violin teacher!"

Since he's Ben's stepfather, I let it all out. I tell him the story of how I ended up in a tent to get away from people.

"I read about cha in the newspapuh. Youa da famous kid dat disappeaed. What a small woild."

When I tell him that Thomas Harrison is my stepfather, Johnny Accardo's eyes widen. He says, "Youa step fatha is Thomas Harrison, dat rich guy dats tryin ta fix ouha faia city? Da guy dat has it all togetha? Wit a minista like Benny, a violin techea like Savich, and a billionaina step fatha like Thomas Harrison, what da hell ah you doin' livin' in a fuckin' tent?"

I tell him the story of how I wanted to get away from everyone bothering me etcetera, etcetera.

"Let me tell ya a story. When I was a kid, I was a golden gloves boxa in Madison Squaah Gaaden. I loint one ting. Don't just stand dare when you see a glove comin at cha. You gotta roll wit da punches, kid, or dey'll knock ya out every time. Benny got knocked out a lot right heha in Portland, as a minista, no less. He leoint how to take em down. Whateva he loint, was betta dan boxin. He don't even give em a chance to take a hit. He's a good boy. Say hi to him foa me. I miss him. We don't see much of each otha lately. He's got a lot on his hands. His choich boint down. Assholes ah afta him. He has a new dalin baby goil, da prettiest ting in the woild. You should heah his beautiful wife, Alex, play da violin. She plays a knockout blow to any heavyweight playa."

"I have heard her play; she's my violin teacher—remember?"

"Oh dats right, I fagot. I gotta go take a pee kid, I'll be right back."

I sit here pondering how ironic it is to meet Ben's stepfather. We didn't talk about his cancer.

When Johnny returns, he says, "God damn pastate gland. Makes me pee all da time—especially afta a cup of coffee."

I ask Johnny, "Does Ben know about your cancer?"

"Hell no. He'd stop everyting he's got goin ta help me out. His foist wife died of canca you know. He don't need to worry about me wit fuckin' canca."

"Shit," I say to myself. "Should I tell Ben what's going on with his stepfather or keep it to myself?"

"Nice meetin' ya, kid. Whad ya say youa name was?"

"Theo," I answer.

"Dats right, I fagot. Say hi to Benny for me. Will ya?"

"Sure," I say.

If I contact Ben, it will blow my cover. I've got some heavy-duty thinking to do about the awful situation I have myself in. Johnny gets a taxi for a ride home.

While walking back to my tent, it's getting cold and windy as night approaches. I didn't wear my Peace Through Global Domination hoodie to the VA for fear that it may be offensive to Veterans. When I return to my tent, I look for my hoodie to keep warm, but it's gone. Someone had stolen it.

17. She Was Just Thirty-Seven

I remember seeing her outside the Arlene Schnitzer Concert Hall after Portland Youth Philharmonic concerts. She was always on the corner with her two children asking for money. I could hardly stand seeing this. The Heathman Hotel Restaurant is next door to the Arlene Schnitzer Concert Hall entrance. The first time we attempted to dine there after a concert, you could see cold and hungry people on the sidewalk through the vast table-side picture windows. Emma begged Thomas to leave. So, Thomas, after pondering the situation with his newfound wealth, starts up a homeless program. He's donating most of his wealth to it pledging nearly a billion dollars to be doubled, dollar for dollar, with donations. He names his homeless program Emma's Wish. I was so busy practicing that I didn't even process what he was up to. What a coincidence that the same people Emma cried over are now my neighbors, and my stepfather is attempting to fix the problem.

I see their tent several blocks from mine. Out of curiosity, I walk towards it.

"Mom, I'm hungry," says the young boy sitting outside the tent.

"Me too," says the younger girl.

"Don't worry." She pulls out of her shopping cart two Portland Rescue Mission paper bags full of food.

"Where do you all sleep at night?" I ask.

"We all sleep on the floor of a gymnasium at the shelter. They give us foam mattresses and sleeping bags."

She looks at me with wide-open, full brown eyes.

She says, "No person or child should get used to being homeless. It's not okay; it's hard times. They wake us up at 6:30 in the morning. I get their clothes on. And then we head out towards the bus and go to school. I don't think my youngest son understands that he's homeless. It's dark outside when we walk to the bus. I have no vehicle. I have no income."

"Where did you grow up?"

"Guam. My father wanted me to come out here. I met my husband, Christopher, and fell in love with him. I lost a lot of things with him. So, I divorced him and started a new life with my kids. We live in this tent during the day. Every morning, after getting these two on the school bus, I go to my father's apartment, where three more of my children live."

"You have five children?"

"God gave me all five of my beautiful children. I'm a good Catholic, where birth control is a sin."

I think to myself, Birth control is a sin. Isn't it a sin to have five children you can't care for? This makes no sense to me at all.

"I've been homeless for the last three years. I stayed with my family. I've stayed in hotels. I've been in shared shelters. Three years ago, I was employed at an Albertsons bakery. I keep my head up; I keep my faith. I look forward to finding housing. Living life is so hard. We love and care for people. We love each other. I don't know how to get angry."

She lights a cigarette.

"I want to cry, scream, and talk to God. My kids are a gift of life. They keep me going. We can play foosball at the shelter. They have showers there. Lights out at 8:30. We sleep on the gym floor with foam mattresses. They give us blankets too. Survival is to stay strong and believe in my church."

I offer her a Street Smarts booklet. "Oh, I have one of those. That's how I found out about the safe gymnasium floor we sleep on at night."

I walk away feeling helpless to do anything and nothing but hopelessness for this family. I'm amazed that there are churches that don't allow birth control yet don't mind if families must live like they force her to live. Even if I gave her all my money, she'd still be in the same situation she's in now, and I would have no funds at all. There are hundreds if not thousands of people who live like this. Emma's wish is becoming more and more meaningful as I experience homelessness hell. They should at least pass out free condoms.

18. Where Are My Jewels?

It's raining at dusk, and I can hear the out-of-tune train horn blast its way through the conglomeration of warehouses and bridges. Lined up and down the streets are hundreds of tents. Emma works at the Oregon Museum of Science and Industry, south of my tent, running a planetarium show. She doesn't know that my tent is within walking distance from OMSI. Today, I walk in the rain to OMSI and sneak into her show. She doesn't notice me; the room is pitch black with nothing but the sky showing on the giant dome. She's brilliant, explaining the vastness of the universe while mesmerizing kids and adults. Thomas once told me he used to attend the OMSI planetarium presentations when it was next to the Portland Zoo on the west side of Portland. He said they had a giant two-story pendulum that swung back and forth in the museum. They would set up pegs, in a circle, around the pendulum, and as it swung back and forth, it would knock down a peg every few minutes. The pendulum doesn't rotate; but the ground underneath it does, which proves that the earth is spinning around on its axis and takes one day.

She asks all the kids in the room to stand and jump once. "Why did you come down?" she asks. "Gravity," she answers.

While looking at a picture of the Milky Way projected on the planetarium dome, Emma explains how gravity works. "The most extreme example of gravity in the known universe is a supermassive black hole from which nothing, not even light, can escape. Supermassive black holes have masses that are over one million suns together."

All the kids ooh and awe when she says this.

"Scientists have proved that every large galaxy has a supermassive black hole at its center. The supermassive black hole at the center of the Milky Way Galaxy, of which Earth is a part, is called Sagittarius A, with a mass of about four million suns. We can't even imagine this amount of gravity. It's hard enough to understand why when you jump, you come down rather than going up."

Emma continues to enthrall everyone in the room, including adults. She'll be attending Yale in the fall as an astrophysics major. If I don't emerge from hiding, she'll probably postpone her matriculation looking for me. I must decide. Everyone's looking for me. I'm ruining people's lives because of my self-pity. Poor Claire. Her parents will only pay for Bob Jones University or Liberty University—two of the most conservative fundamentalist Christian universities in the country. With the extreme wealth of her parents, she can't get a need-based scholarship. She won a merit-based scholarship to Linfield University in McMinnville, Oregon, studying theater and communication arts. She can't postpone this scholarship. If she did so for my sake, I couldn't live with myself. I need to get out of this hellhole and make a U-Turn. Making the best of my daymares is what I will have to do. I decide to return home and get my act together.

When I walk back to my tent, thinking about the changes I must make in my life, the 'bad dude' Dick Wolf bursts out of his tent before I enter my tent wielding a baseball bat.

"Where are my jewels, asshole?"

"What jewels?" I ask.

"My jewels, you little fucker. I stored them in the drainpipe behind your tent. They're gone."

I remember him lifting the bat. That's all I remember.

When I come out of a fog in the hospital, Claire's at my bedside.

"Theo," she cries, "Thank God you're alive."

She takes my hand and puts her head next to mine and lifts her head with a tear-soaked smile on her face. Mom, Thomas, Ben, and Alex are all wiped out on chairs in the hospital room. They wake up when they hear Claire. They get up and surround me at my bedside.

Mom says, "Thank God you're awake."

Thomas says, "We love you, Theo."

Ben says, "You're a champ."

In a fog, I ask, "What happened? My head hurts like hell. It's all bandaged up."

Claire says, "Ben and I were riding around your neighborhood, looking for you, on his Harley. We found you face down, out cold, laying on the sidewalk and called an ambulance."

My eyes come into focus. Ben's standing there in a leather jacket and leather pants.

I look at Claire, who's wearing cargo pants and groggily ask, "Were you riding with Ben on his Harley Davidson beast?"

"Yep," she says proudly.

I say, "Ben took me on a ride to Mt. Tabor to teach me a lesson about how stupid he is. Was he trying to teach you a lesson too?"

"No. We were looking for you."

I feel guilty. I knew my stupid selfishness would eventually involve people who love me.

I ask, "Were you wearing a helmet?"

"Of course, I was wearing a helmet, you stupid klutz."

"As I recall, Dick Wolf, the guy living in the tent next to mine, steaming mad and wielding a baseball bat, said something about jewels before the lights went out."

Claire says, "Could have been Dick Wolf. When he attempted to get the jewels, he must have stolen, they were gone. The police found the jewels behind your tent in a drainpipe and took them when you weren't there; they were looking for you."

Emma continues with urgency, "Surveillance cameras saw someone break the glass of a jewelry store and steal the jewels in the window. He was wearing a hoodie that said on the back, 'Peace Through Global Domination.' They think it was your hoodie, and that you stole the jewels!"

"Dick Wolf must have been the thief who stole my hoodie. I loved that thing. I wanted to ask my father about it, as they made it in Olongapo City, Philippines."

Mom says, "The police think you were wearing the jacket because the homeless store that gives away clothes identified you as the guy who bought it."

"So, the police think it was me, but Dick Wolf stole my jacket and wore it when he robbed the jewelry store. What a revolting development."

Thomas says, "When you can walk, they'll take you to jail to await a hearing."

I'm fully awake now. "What? Jail? God, my head hurts."

Thomas continues, "Don't worry, Theo, we have your back."

"How do you all propose to do that?"

Ben says, "Remember, Theo, Detective Jeremy Smith, and Lizzy figured out who burned the church down. Jeremy's already on the case. When the police interview you, tell them you have representation; and say nothing else."

"Okay," I say.

I try to get up but can't.

Claire holds out the undershirt I was wearing since leaving home with two fingers, "Do you mind if we take your sickening old smelly undershirt?"

"What for?"

"Jeremy, Ben, Lizzy, and I will investigate the crime scene. Jeremy wants to explore the neighborhood with Lizzy's infamous olfactory glands."

"Claire, it's not a very safe neighborhood."

"Don't worry; I have some protection."

"What protection?"

Claire reaches into one of her cargo pants pockets and pulls out this thing she puts into her hand. Sharp steel spikes protrude in between her fingers.

"This is my tiger claw. Belle Brown, Ben's self-defense instructor, now gives me self-defense lessons and requires that I have this with me at all times."

"You were looking for me in Tent City wearing cargo pants wielding steel claws between your fingers?"

"Theo," Mom says, "The entire church has been looking for you, not just in tent cities in Portland, but on the internet and everywhere you might look for missing persons. Jeremy has the best intelligence, and from it, we narrowed you down to the neighborhood they found you in."

I lament to everyone, "I feel terrible about all this. I just wanted to get away from everybody and figure things out, because I can't play the violin anymore, so I needed some time. Ironically, homeless neighbors and a baseball bat have helped me figure things out. Either that or I'm really stupid—like Ben. I need to tell you all a story."

I tell them the story of Ben at the grocery store and not calling 911 etcetera, and how stupid he is.

"He's right. I shouldn't have moved into a stupid tent just to get away from people."

"Yeah, that was stupid of you, Theo." Claire agrees.

"It sure was," Ben also agrees. "Hopefully, you will learn from your stupidity, as I did."

I heard little else, as the medication made me fall asleep.

19. Discovery and Investigation

I call Jeremy Smith.

He answers, "Hi Ben, what's up?"

"Do you have any news about Theo?" I ask.

"Of course, I do. We found a sleeping bag and an air mattress in his tent. He was wearing his backpack when Dick Wolf assaulted him; in it he had hand-written notes on musical staff paper. All this is under lock and key in my office."

"Looks like Theo was writing music," I say. "Also, a police officer is guarding the door of Theo's hospital room."

"They'll arrest him as soon as he can walk," Jeremy tells me.

"What do we do?" I ask.

"It's simple. We go to Tent City and look for clues. I'll pick you up tomorrow at six a.m. sharp."

"Sounds good," I confirm.

"Meanwhile, you need to tell Theo to keep his mouth shut when they read him his Miranda rights."

"I already told him this," I confirm. "We have several attorneys in our church who'd love to represent Theo."

Jeremy says, "By the time we gather evidence, I suspect they will acquit Theo before needing a lawyer. I'm sure we can find out who did it with Lizzy, Theo's clothes, you, and Claire."

"On another subject, Alex tells me you and Carla are doing well. She won't say much else for fear of breaking confidence."

"We're in somewhat of a dilemma. Carla lives in Boston; I live in Portland. One of us must move, or we'll both go broke. If we want to continue with this intoxicating relationship, I'll have to find a job in Boston, or she'll have to find a job in Portland."

"Is it leaning one way or the other?"

"I already know the Chief of Police in Boston. She helped me investigate Palmer Grandstone's possible role in your church fire. If an opening existed, I could get a job as a detective in the Boston police. Carla has it made in Boston with her job as principal oboe in the Boston Symphonic. It would be harder for her to move to Portland."

"But" I add, "It would thrill Alex to have her best friend living here in Portland. She misses her greatly."

"Ben, Palmer is as fixated on Carla as he was on Alex before she got pregnant. He shows up at concerts and 'accidentally' bumps into her all around town and sends her expensive flowers weekly. He's a menace."

"Does she ever tell him to back off?"

"No matter what she does, he won't leave her alone. He has done nothing illegal and law enforcement can't charge him with stalking by sending her flowers and having chance encounters. To get him for stalking, she'd have to prove that he threatened her with obscene phone calls, emails, or letters. Most studies show stalkers stop when their target is no longer available to them or find someone else to harass. Palmer is smart enough to keep his distance but lets her know she's always on his mind."

"It makes sense that she should consider moving to Portland as long as Palmer makes her life miserable. If you went to Boston, he would still be there. He's tenacious from what Alex went through, and 'no' means 'yes' to him. Do you mind if I talk to Alex about your dilemma?"

"Please do. Perhaps we can all come up with a solution together."

Meanwhile, today, I have a sermon to write, three counseling appointments, and a church council meeting tonight. I take Honey for a ride; she helps me write sermons. Sometimes sermons will pop into my head while feeling the wind in my face. We ride around in some of the homeless camps in Portland. The next sermon embeds itself in my mind: "The Inhumanity of Humanity." To allow this to happen is inhumane. Do these people choose to live like this, or are they forced to? Tent cities are springing up all over Portland and other large cities. What's wrong with our capitalist system? How can people live comfortably in upscale neighborhoods like Lake Oswego, yet others live in squalor? Emma's wish is becoming a bit of a big deal.

I say to myself, "I don't do many Christocentric sermons, but I'll expound this Sunday on Matthew 25:40: "And the King will answer and say to them, Assuredly, I say to you, since you did *it* to one of the least of these My brethren, you did *it* to Me."

I drive Honey home and continue with my busy day.

20. Jail for Theo

Two police officers come into the hospital room and read me my rights when I can finally walk. When the cuffs go on, freedom is gone.

"You're under arrest for grand theft. You have the right to remain silent. Anything you say can and will be used against you in a court of law. You have the right to an attorney. If you can't afford an attorney, one will be provided. Do you understand the rights I have just read to you? Do you wish to speak to me with these rights in mind?"

I do what Ben advised me to do. I say that I have representation and say nothing else. When we arrive at the jail, the intake process begins.

"Take your shoes off."

I comply.

"Do you have any dependency problems?"

"No."

"Do you take any medications?"

"No."

"Have you attempted suicide?"

"No."

They fingerprint me and take a mugshot.

I'm escorted to the shower room; when we arrive, the guard says, "Strip."

I comply.

A beefy-looking guard stands there while I shower, watching me as if I would commit a crime in the shower. After I shower with a delouser, I put on a scratchy orange jumpsuit. I'm not allowed to wear any underwear.

They put me in an eight-by-six-foot room that smells like the toilet, which sits prominently in the center of the wall. I carry my disinfected plastic mattress into the room and put it on the metal rack. They give me sheets and a scratchy wool blanket. There's a metal mirror on the wall, but it's all scratched up, so you can't see yourself in it. The stainless-steel sink is part of the toilet. It's boring in here. There's nothing to read but the County Regulations and Disciplinary Code Book. It's even more boring than the official manual on making french fries at McDanny's. There are no windows; the only artwork was what other inmates scratched into the cement block walls.

The guard shoves a plate into the slot in my door.

"Here's your lunch," he says.

It's on a blue plastic plate with indentations for the food consisting of corn, applesauce, and white bread—no butter. To drink is a cup of weak lukewarm tea. It all tastes like the toilet smells, but I put the food in my mouth anyway simply to fill my stomach.

Finally, after a stormy night's sleep, someone pays my bond. The guard hands me my clothes and tells me to put them on. I sign a bond receipt. Thomas is standing in the lobby waiting for me. He hugs me, and I gratefully hug him back.

The biggest thing on my mind is my Blast manuscript. I ask him, "What happened to the stuff in my tent and my backpack?"

He tells me, "It's all under lock and key in Jeremy's office as evidence."

"Did he mention some handwritten music in my backpack?"

"Yep."

"Will I ever see it again?"

"Yep."

"When?"

"You'll get your stuff, eventually. Were you writing some music?"

I answer, "Just some doodling."

21. Dickhoff's Vision

"Hi, my name is Natalie Schrunk. I'm the head of the Lake Oswego High School LGBTQ Alliance. We're gathered today to support each other, as we're not 'straight.' I've been the victim of discrimination in countless ways since coming out. We need to become active in supporting LGBTQ students. In Lake Oswego, we have a church spreading disinformation and actively working to disenfranchise all of you of your sexual identity. They're also traumatizing LGBTQ high school students forced to go there with their parents—as I once was. The Lake Oswego Fundamentalist Church of America, FUCA needs to hear from every one of us. Pastor Gerard Dickhoff hates you. He and his church are profiting from their bigotry and LGBTQ phobia with their gay conversion program. I'll be leading this delegation of LGBTQ students to one of their services. They used to have a famous sign that read: 'Tired of Sin? Come In.' I wrote in red lipstick, 'If not, dial 503-555-1125.' It made the news headlines, as some may recall. Please show up at this so-called church next Sunday at 9:45 a.m. They remember me as a grade-school boy wearing pants. I'm older and don't look like that anymore, so they probably won't recognize me."

We show up at 9:45 Sunday in the narthex, and a smiley woman, who I remember well, greets us. She's especially thrilled to see new young impressionable high school students.

"Hi, welcome to the Lake Oswego Fundamentalist Church of America. We've seen none of you here before. You seem like friendly, well-dressed kids."

The woman points to me and says, "What a cute dress."

"Thank you," I say.

Do you all attend Lake Oswego High School?"

Everyone says, "Yes."

"Have you heard of the Four Spiritual Laws?"

Everyone says, "No."

"You all have a lot to learn about God. Here is a pamphlet that will show you the Way, the Truth, and the Life."

We all take a copy and smile.

They're four hymns that we're supposed to sing during the service. The guy sitting next to me asks, "Don't you love these hymns? This is what it will be like in heaven—singing hymns about Jesus."

The first verse of the hymn right before the sermon hymn is:

What can wash away my sin?
Nothing but the blood of Jesus.
What can make me whole again?
Nothing but the blood of Jesus.

They sing the refrain four times after each verse.

O precious is the flow
that makes me white as snow;
no other fount I know;
nothing but the blood of Jesus.

I ask the guy sitting next to me, "Is there a lot of blood in heaven?"

The guy takes a while to answer me.

Finally, he snarls, "The blood of Jesus was shed for you and me, period. You don't need to question this fact. Accept it or burn in hell. There is only one way to God—by the blood of Jesus."

The congregation sings three more verses of this wretched hymn. It brings back traumatizing memories of my childhood.

Next comes the highly anticipated sermon. Dickhoff yells and screams and pounds his fist on the pulpit. He appears to be angry and hateful of everything except for his religious worldview. He is such a biblical literalist, that he probably believes that the earth is flat.

He ends by proclaiming, "Homosexuals are an abomination. They'd mortify our foundin' fathers. These sinners are destroyin' our Godly country."

An Alliance member stands up and yells:

"Founding fathers? Our founding fathers were grown men wearing wigs, heels, rouge, and silk stockings."

"Shut-up pervert! Our foundin' fathers gave us the precious blood-a-Jesus!"

"No, they didn't. They came here to get away from Jesus. Read the First Amendment to the Constitution. Most of them were deists!"

"Security, escort this unruly pervert outa our sacred space. As the hymn clearly saith, nothin' but the blood-a-Jesus can save the gays. He shed his blood for them, but they defy His sacrifice, mainly by their perverted sexual desires and proclivities. One such place in Lake Oswego that supports the gay lifestyle is The Lake Oswego Progressive Church of America, led by the Reverend Dr. Ben Dawson; this place is a den of iniquity, not a sacred Godly church like ours. Men with long hair caked with makeup are holding hands and wearin' skirts. Women with short hair and no makeup are wearin' pants. It's a God damnable abomination. They don't mention the blood of Jesus in this den of iniquity. In fact, they don't even believe in the Bible as God's sacred, infallible holy word. This place is the devil's playground! They're all gonna burn in hell!!!" He hangs on to the word hell forever until he runs out of breath.

Several LGBTQ Alliance hands go up in the congregation:

"I'm a lesbian. Am I going to hell?"

"I'm gay. Am I going to hell?"

"I'm bisexual. Am I going to hell?"

"I'm transgender. Am I going to hell?"

"I'm asexual. Am I going to hell?"

"I'm pansexual. Am I going to hell?"

"How dare you interrupt my sermon! But yes, you're all goin' to hell if you don't repent and attend this church."

"But only one of us is gay."

"It don't matter. You're all 'people of the gay,' and if you don't repent, I shudder to think of what'll happen to you when you die. Hell is a terrible place for sexual perverts. The only legitimate sex is between a man and woman, equally yoked together in Christian matrimony for the sole purpose of makin'-a-baby. Any other sexual activity is an abomination!"

Another wonderful LGBTQ Alliance member asks, "Are rape and incest abominations?"

Dickhoff fumes, "Abortion is an abomination! Incense? What does incense have to do with anythin'? The only people lightin' up incense are Catholics, Buddists, Hindus and hippies. The smoke makes 'em high and diverts their attention away from the blood of Jesus. Rape is God's will to make babies. Women who get raped have to forgive their rapists; it's the Godly thing to do. Rapists aren't to blame when women wear skirts above their knees, skintight tank tops, and bottoms, and way too much make up. Women deserve to get raped when they entice men like little sex devils.

Only I can save you all. I can do it individually if you join our church and start tithin', or you can take part in our highly affordable gay conversion program when you turn eighteen."

"Amen, highly affordable," the congregation proclaims in unison.

"If you're not interested in salvation by the blood-a-Jesus and conversion, please leave now. If not, I'll have security escort you heathens out-a-here."

While they escort us out, we chant in unison, "Glory to wigs, heels, rouge, and silk stockings. Glory to wigs, heels, rouge, and silk stockings...."

22. Theo Is in Jail

"Claire Devine. Theo Hall is in jail." My fuming mother is interrogating me. "He's in jail suspected of grand theft!"

I just finished a grueling training session with Belle. I shouldn't have come home. All I want to do is go to bed and crash. I'm wiped out.

"Why, it's in the newspaper that Thomas Harrison's stepson, Theo Hall, is in jail. I told you not to associate with those atheist democrat communist lowlife criminal perverts! What do you have to say for yourself, young lady?"

My mom doesn't know what I endured looking for Theo, finding him lying on the sidewalk, and seeing him in the hospital. I'm thrilled we found him, but the circumstances couldn't be worse. I don't want to be rude and sarcastic around my mom, but it's hard to contain myself after what she just said.

I tell her as calmly as I can, "Theo and his family are wonderful people. If Theo's in jail, it's entirely a big mistake. I want to go to my room. I'm tired."

Mom continues angrily, "The newspaper said that Theo Hall lived in a tent near the railroad tracks on the east side of the river. What was he doing there? Is he a drug addict? Why are you wearing such ugly clothes? Cargo pants? What do you know about all this?"

"Mom, I don't want to talk about it."

"You will talk about it now, young lady! Also, Pastor Dickhoff thinks Theo's gay."

"Why would he think this?" I ask.

"Because he likes classical music, has devoted his life to an instrument only girls play, and doesn't like sports—like real men. Pastor Dickhoff has a unique understanding of gay perverts. He specializes in converting them to what God intended men to be."

"Are you serious? That's the most ridiculous thing I've ever heard in my life. Dickhoff is a homophobic pig. I hate him. How could you possibly give money to his church?"

"Claire, your mouth is becoming an instrument of the devil. How dare you swear at me!"

I walk up the grand staircase to my bedroom.

"Why are you tired?" my mom yells. "Are you drinking from the same cup as your 'liberal' friends? Claire, if you don't have Jesus in your heart and love him with all your heart, soul, and mind, the devil and his friends! will victimize you!"

Mom cries like a river.

"Mom, I'm sorry, but I don't buy into fundamentalist Christianity. I'm not a fan of pastor Dickhoff and his gay conversion therapy program. I know you like to hang out with your rich fundamentalist evangelical Republican friends at the Exclusive River Country Club, and I know fully that you want Fred Freemark and me to date, but I just can't do it, mom. Since I have to make my own way through college, even though you guys could help me with any college in the world, except for the only two colleges that reflect Dickhoff's vision, I'm doing it on my own. I'm sorry, but I'll find my own path."

"Claire, you do not know how embarrassed we'll be when people find out you're cavorting with criminals. We may not even be able to show our faces at the country club. You will lose the support of Fred Freemark's parents if you continue to associate with low-life criminals!"

I say calmly, "Mom, your friends at the Exclusive River Country Club, unlike low life criminals, are high-life criminals. They look down on everyone if they're not rich and flaunt their wealth with big expensive homes and fancy cars. Most of them steal from the poor and give it to themselves. They are all jealous of each other too. As for your friends at FUCA, they have a narrow view of the world and think that everyone should believe what they believe, or they will go to hell. In addition to placing themselves above everyone with their wealth, they place themselves far above everyone else with their exclusive, bigoted religious beliefs. I'm eighteen and will be on my own soon so you won't have to be bothered with me anymore."

My mother stands there, silently staring at me in disbelief. This is the first time I have spoken to her this way. I'm surprised she didn't throw me out of the house. I close my door, lock it, flop down on my bed, and fall fast asleep.

23. Tiger Lady

Ben wakes me up with a phone call. "Claire, I thought I'd let you know we will look for evidence tomorrow into who bludgeoned Theo. Jeremy wants to be there at 6:00 in the morning. Lizzy and her magnificent nose for news will go with us."

I groggily reply, "Can you pick me up at the Riverdale Grade School parking lot at 5:30?"

"See you then," Ben affirms.

I set my alarm for 5:00 and sneak out of the house. My tiger claw is in one of the many pockets of my cargo pants. I make it to the parking lot on time, pumped up and ready to find out who bludgeoned Theo.

When we arrive at where we found Theo, there's only one lone tent. Dick Wolf's tent is gone, and Theo's former tent stands alone. Jeremy, Ben, Lizzy, and I poke our heads inside. It's empty.

Ben says, "I can't believe Theo's tent is still here, and no one has occupied it yet."

Jeremy remarks with streetwise wisdom, "It's only been a day. Give it a few more hours; the tent will be gone, or someone else will occupy it."

Jeremy and Lizzy go snooping around the neighborhood with Theo's old tee shirt.

Ben says, "I need a cup of coffee, and I'd like to ask a few questions about Dick Wolf in the coffee shop around the block to see if anyone knows anything. I'll be right back. Do you want anything?"

"A cup of coffee would be fine," I say.

I go into the empty tent and sit there thinking about what it must have been like for Theo. Everyone's looking for him. Anyone who knew anything about where he lived, including the media, hounded him. They wouldn't leave him alone when he lived with his parents, so he ended up here. This stinking cold tent is probably the only place he could find peace when he lived in it. I wonder what I would have done. I can't stand living with my parents, but I need to go to college and can't afford to live independently. My parents think I'm the devil because I went to the prom with Theo, and they live in Dunthorpe. I'd rather live in this tent with Theo than with my parents in their ostentatious mansion. God, it stinks in here. Well, maybe I would rather live in this tent with Theo than in an ostentatious mansion; I'm not that stupid. Theo is my favorite person. I've loved him forever. When I saw his gleaming eyes in second grade, I wanted to kiss him. He didn't know how cute he was, how talented he was, and how sensitive and friendly he was. We were just kids, and Theo was simply adorable. He ignored me for the longest time. I would purposely get in his way in the hall at school, and he would apologize for getting in my way. Why am I crying? He was always such a gentleman. Countless boys have always attempted to get my attention, but the only boy that has ever gotten my attention is Theo, even though he never tried—dammit.

As I look around the tent, it's barren—just musty canvas walls. Theo's tent isn't a fancy-colored modern fabric tent; it's an old green smelly canvas one. There's a flap that covers a zipper. It looks well worn. I open it with my finger and discover a small picture of me that Theo took when we walked on a bridge at Elk Rock Garden near my home. All the same old feelings come flooding back when I discover this picture of me. Perhaps he was thinking of me. I put the picture in my cargo pants pocket, and just melted there like a puddle of pudding and wept even more. I couldn't stop thinking of Theo.

The tent door swings open, and a strange-looking man enters. He's skinny and tall. His face has weathered wrinkles, and his teeth are brown like he hadn't brushed them in years. He tattooed on his neck a Skull and Crossbones. Seeing my tears, he smiles.

"Hey, little lady. I saw you when you got inside Bob's old tent. Pleased to meet you. What's with the tears? Do you miss little Bobby?"

"Who's Bobby?" I ask. "Who are you?"

"You must know the little fucker. You're cryin' in his tent."

He's blocking the door, so I can't run away. So, while he's talking, I reach for my tiger claw in my cargo pants.

"Here, I'll help you get over him."

He pulls down his pants and pushes me to the ground. I clench my fist around my tiger claw. He was about to discover that no one messes with this Tiger Lady. I replace my tears with blood lust.

"Hey, little girl, I'll bet you never had a real man take care of you."

All my training with Belle kicks in—like I'm on automatic pilot. When his hand is busy fumbling with his penis, I scratch his eye with my tiger claw as hard as I can just as Belle had taught me to do with practice dummies. His revolting penis disappears like a turtle's head shrinking into its shell.

"What the fuck, bitch! Who do you think you are? I'm bleedin'—my eye, my eye!"

He attempts to hit me. I block his hand, and with all the force I can muster, I kick him in the crotch. He doubles over in pain. I'm glad I wore my heavy-duty hiking boots today. He falls to the ground and lays there groaning in pain and struggles somehow to get his feet. He leaves the tent bloodied, bruised, and screaming in pain. I'm traumatized but somehow pumped that I can defend myself. Thank you, Belle!

I yell at him as he limps away, "I'm your worst enemy, asshole!"

We practiced this scenario countless times at the police training center, and as Theo would always say, "Practice makes perfect."

Walking toward the tent, Ben holds two cups of coffee; he hears me yelling at my unlucky attacker. Shaking, I have a triumphant smile on my face, and my tiger claw, still in my hand, is dripping with blood.

"What happened? Who's an asshole?" Ben worriedly asks.

"The guy who lived next to Theo paid a brief visit. He called Theo, 'Bob.'"

"Oh my God," Ben gasps. "We never should have taken you down here—ever."

"Ben," I say, "don't worry; you and I have the same self-defense instructor."

Ben can't argue with me; he hands me a hot cup of coffee.

Jeremy and Lizzy show up at the tent. Jeremy has the famous Peace Through Global Domination hoodie and the bat. He's equally concerned about what happened to me as Ben is.

"Are you okay?" Jeremy asks.

"I'm not only okay, but I'm also pumped." I take a sip of coffee with my left hand, lifting my right hand with the blood-soaked tiger claw. "If this is the creep who bludgeoned Theo, I hope he goes blind! Damn, this coffee is good."

Jeremy's mind is spinning, "As bad as this is, we now have blood samples of the broken glass that the robber must have cut himself on, DNA from this coat, DNA from the bat, and DNA from the attempted rapist himself on your tiger claw."

Jeremy carefully takes my claw and puts it into a plastic bag.

"Ben, why didn't you get me a cup of coffee?" asks Jeremy.

"I only have two hands," Ben replies.

"How did you find Theo's coat?" I ask.

"Lizzy." Jeremy replies, "She could smell Theo from the scent of his tee-shirt, and when she led me to a dumpster, I had the revolting dis-pleasure of dumpster diving. The coat has blood splatter on it, and the bat has bloodstains on it where it presumably hit Theo's head. We're in fat-city with evidence. All we must do is find Dick Wolf, arrest him, and the rest will be only a bad dream that's over."

"How do we find Dick Wolf?" I ask—still pumped with adrenaline and now caffeine from the coffee.

"Did you get a good look at him?" Jeremy asks.

"There's no way I couldn't remember a face like that. He's a tall skinny guy with a weather-beaten face, crooked brown teeth, and skull and crossbones tattooed on his ugly neck. He wasn't circumcised either."

Ben chimes in, "At the coffee shop, the barista described a guy matching that description, except for his penis, who would come in now and then wearing Theo's, Peace Through Global Domination, hoodie. He bragged recently about finding a better place to put his tent. He said it was a much nicer location, underneath the Morrison Bridge overpasses, out of the rain, and further away from the train tracks."

"Well done," said Jeremy. "Looks like we may find the guy who nearly killed Theo. Who knows what he could have done to you, Claire."

I finally shudder, thinking about what could have happened, but knowing that I can defend myself, I feel empowered.

Jeremy continues, "We have all the blood evidence we need; we need you, Claire, to ID him. Time is of the essence. I must assemble some officers to go with us."

"Ben, I'll pick you up at 9:45."

"Aye, aye, captain," Ben replies.

"Claire, can you meet us in the grade school parking lot at ten a.m. tomorrow?"

"I'll be there," I enthusiastically affirm.

24. Crime Scene Investigation and Arrest

The next day at 9:30 am, I put on my trusty cargo pants, heavy hiking boots, and an old shirt; I sneak out of the house and walk to the school parking lot. I feel like a hardened undercover police investigator looking for the perp. Jeremy pulls up in his black SUV with Ben inside. Ben's wearing his usual clothes—cargo pants and a flannel shirt. He looks like he lives in Tent City usually. Jeremy's dressed up as if he lives down there as well. We're all undercover snoops. I almost feel like this is more fun than stage acting. It's the real thing.

Jeremy gleefully states, "All the samples match one person except where the bat hit Theo's head. Theo's blood is on the bat at the spot where it hit him, but not on the coat or the glass from the window."

When we arrive under the Southeast Morrison Street overpasses, we meet two police cars with two uniformed officers; one is Belle, my new BFF and self-defense instructor, and a guy named Officer Drummond.

Belle gives me a new tiger claw. "After what you went through, you deserve this."

"Thanks," I say. "I'll never leave home without it."

Jeremy says, "Let's go for a walk. Officers Drummond and Brown will follow about a block behind us."

Belle smiles at me and says, "Let's get the SOB."

I could tell that Belle knows the type of guy we're after and wants him to be brought to justice as badly as I do.

We walk around the neighborhood. The entire experience mortifies me. As my parents think, are these people just lazy, or as Thomas thinks, do they need help and rehabilitation? Countless people are smoking pot openly. Some people just sit on the sidewalk doing nothing. Some are shooting up drugs with needles right out in the open. Some are just sleeping on the sidewalk. Blankets are covering a hunched over woman; her head looks helplessly down at the sidewalk. We walk past piles of stinking garbage, feces, and hypodermic needles. I see a rat scurry under an old box. A car pulls up to a red light, and a woman lifts her dress and urinates on the street in front of the stopped vehicle. It's hard to tell if the tents are empty or occupied. People of all ages are living here. Some can hardly walk, others look alone and scared, and others dance to boom boxes. From a police photo Jeremy has, we can see several tents that look like Dick Wolf's tent.

Jeremy asks me to stand back while he says to the occupants of tents that look like Wolf's, "Is anybody in there?"

Sometimes, someone will poke their head out of the tent, and it isn't Dick Wolf. I show to Jeremy and the officers following us, thumbs down, that it isn't Wolf. At one tent that looks like Wolf's, no one answers, but I see him walking towards this tent; it must be his. He has a patch on his right eye. I put my thumb up and point to him with my other hand. When Wolf sees us at his tent, he runs. Ben's closest to him; he tackles him to the ground, puts his hands behind his back and holds them with his face down. He's no match for the buffed-up pastor. Ben has a triumphant grin that belies his status as a minister. He looks more like a beefed-up undercover cop who just nailed the bad guy. Belle and Drummond rush up to him and put handcuffs on him.

Jeremy says, "You're under arrest for grand theft, assault, and attempted rape." He reads him his rights.

Wolf, squirming from the constraints, says, "Prove it motherfuckers. You're violatin' my first amendment rights. That fuckin' bitch over there blinded me in my right eye. She should be in handcuffs, not me!"

"Don't worry about that," Jeremy says back. "We have enough evidence to put you in a secure place where you don't have to worry about your rights. They will care for your little eye boo-boo as well. Although, you'll have to watch your back in prison."

Officer Drummond pulls up in his police car, puts Wolf into the back seat, and takes off. Several people come out of their tents from the confusion looking thrilled with getting Wolf out of the neighborhood.

Looking about my age, a young black girl comes up to us crying and stutters to Belle, "He... he... he...." Belle takes her aside and talks to her for about ten minutes. Belle leaves to get her police car. The girl gets her belongings from her tent, and we stand here with the girl for a spell. She says nothing—like she's in shock; when Belle returns, the girl opens up. Since Belle is black, she probably feels safe with her. She sits in the front seat next to Belle, and the car takes off.

Several people are cheering about what just happened. Many look at us with respect; others quickly return to their tents.

"Let's get out of here," says Jeremy.

Ben looks around the neighborhood and says, "If Emma's Wish can clean up this mess, we'll have a glorious victory on our hands in Portland."

"Amen," I agree.

We walk back to Jeremy's SUV and call it a day.

25. Coffee with Carla, Claire, and Alex

When Carla gave me a free oboe lesson before the rape attempt, she not only helped me with some embouchure issues but gave me some sage advice about love and romance. I'm not sure how it all came up, but talking to an adult, who doesn't judge me like my mother, was fun. During our lesson, I told Carla about Fred Freemark, what an ass he is, how he won't leave me alone, and how my mother wants me to date him. I told her about the prom as well. She advised me to stay away from toxic people. Carla and I became good friends quickly.

Alex asks me if I want to come with her to the airport to pick up Carla. Alex says Carla's coming to Portland to visit Jeremy, her, and me. We pick up Alex at the Portland Airport. On the way back, we stop for coffee at Chuck's Place in Lake Oswego. Ben told Alex and Carla about the rape attempt, and we talked about it for way too long. I change the subject.

"Carla, you look happy and ready to meet your lover," I say.

Carla replies with a smile, "As you know, Jeremy and I are in love; it just happened. Several years ago, he went to Boston to investigate Palmer Grandstone's possible role in LOPCA's church fire. Since I was becoming locally famous from the Red-Hot Dress scandal, Alex put us together by suggesting that Jeremy talk to me about Palmer. Jeremy and I met at a restaurant in Boston, and we fell in love on the first date."

Alex gloats knowingly as the cupid who put them together.

I ask, "What's the Red-Hot Dress scandal?"

Carla clears her throat, "In a nutshell, Alex, Palmer Grandstone, and I grew up together while performing in the Boston Youth Philharmonic. Since then, Palmer fixated on Alex. Much to the disappointment of Palmer, Alex married Ben. As soon as Alex got pregnant, he focused all his attention on me. Palmer asked me out on a date to a place called Legit Seafood; I thought it was just an old friend meetup, but he decided it was an official date. Since he was such a nuisance to Alex, I thought it would be fun to mess with his mind. I wore the now famous Red-Hot Dress outfit that would definitely mess with his mind. I guess I'm devilish. All I wanted was a bowl of fish chowder and water to drink. Instead, he ordered tons of food for both of us, and all I ate was some soup and salad. He ate everything he ordered, including drinking a whole bottle of champagne. The boy I grew up with in the Boston Youth Symphony ended up vomiting on me and my dress. The man isn't fat or a glutton. I think my Red-Hot Dress had a weird effect on him.

People in the restaurant took pictures and videos of the incident. Because Palmer was locally famous as a rich art store owner, the pictures hit the society pages. I then became famous too. The Boston Symphonic wanted me to perform an oboe concerto with the orchestra in my newly dubbed 'Red-Hot Dress.' Tickets sold out, and the Boston Symphonic Orchestra doubled their ticket sales."

Alex chimes in, "The only way you can get rid of Palmer is to get pregnant."

"That's hilarious," I laugh.

I ask, "Where do you suppose he got that weird accent?"

Carla says, "It sounds like a cross between an arrogant British, high church priest, considering a sip of expensive wine before deciding to swallow it, and a rich Southern tele-evangelist politely asking for more money."

Alex says, "In the Boston Youth Philharmonic he was an average clarinet player, with an expensive instrument, but when he spoke, everyone thought he was from another country. He sounded like William F. Buckley, but he was from Boston, like the rest of us."

"Oh well," Carla says, "because of his family's fame and his public display of weirdness at Legit Seafoods, I'm now the second-highest paid orchestra member next to the concertmaster violinist. I would have to give up a prominent position if I came to Portland to be with Jeremy."

She looks at me, "Claire, I'm sure you got to know Jeremy as the great person he is with all you went through in Tent City. Jeremy's the kindest, sweetest person I've ever known."

"I agree," I say, "Jeremy's a kind and sweet person—so is Theo."

Carla adds, "Stay with the sweet ones, avoid the toxic ones, even if they attempt to woo you."

I ask Carla, "What will you do about your long-distance relationship with Jeremy?"

Carla answers, "Palmer has focused all of his perverted attention on me now. He's in my face at every turn, which is one reason to move to Portland. I have a great position in the Boston Symphonic. The Oregon Symphony would have to have an opening for me to move here, or there would have to be an opening in the Boston Police Department for Jeremy to move to Boston. We may go bankrupt flying back and forth until we decide to do something."

I say with heartfelt gratitude, "I haven't been able to talk about how I feel to anyone, but now I can talk to two women who understand. Love is a bitch. I've been in love with Theo since we were ten. However, I can't get his attention to realize what we have. I'm waiting for him to grow up."

"I think Theo would be well worth the wait," says Alex.

I add, "I have another problem with Fred Freemark. He won't leave me alone. My parents and Fred's parents are also besties and hang out at the Exclusive River Country Club, where initiation fees can start at thirty-five thousand dollars plus, and annual dues can be more than the high five figures. My parents could send me to any college in the world in music or theater. Still, they will only send me to Bob Jones or Liberty University, the most conservative fundamentalist evangelical colleges in the world."

"Sounds vexing," says Carla.

"Sounds like a conundrum," says Alex. "Claire, why do you suppose Fred Freemark is so fixated on you?"

"Beats me. Perhaps for the same reason Palmer fixated on you and now on Carla. I won't talk to Fred. But he's always inserting himself into my life."

Carla looks deep in thought, then says, "Do you think he simply wants what he can't have, like Palmer?"

"That's a likely possibility, but more than likely, he wants to one-up Theo, who he thinks is my boyfriend. Come to think of it, should I back off of Theo? The last time I saw him was when he was in the hospital. I haven't heard from him since then. Is he something I want because I can't have him?"

Alex and Carla, saying nothing, look at me as if I made a salient point.

We leave the coffee shop together, but I decide to walk home alone. The thought haunts me as I walk to Dunthorpe that Theo doesn't return my enthusiasm for him. Am I like Palmer and Fred? If so, I need to take a good hard look at myself and decide if I should change things or just cry. I love Theo and would walk over coals for him, but I'm not sure if he would do the same for me. Theo doesn't have the same enthusiasm for me as I have for him. I had to ask him to the prom. I was there for him when he woke up in the hospital. He just takes me for granted. I cried over someone who doesn't appreciate me. Since we were ten, I've been in Theo's face at every turn, and he doesn't even notice. I'm no better than Palmer or Fred. He doesn't return my love—period. I'm a nuisance to Theo. I need to grow up and get out of his stinking canvas tent. The big question is, why did he have the picture of me in his tent? It must have been a mistake. Too bad for you Theo, I'm moving on to better smelling pastures.

26. Palmer Fired from The Boston Arts Council

My phone rings, and I stupidly answer an unknown number, "Carla? This is Palmer."

"Oh shit," I say to myself. He's calling from a number that isn't in my blocked numbers.

"What do you want, Palmer?"

"I have some fantastic news for you and the entire arts community in Boston."

"What news?" I ask.

"The arts community has brought it to my attention that the Boston Symphonic is now the 'hottest' symphony in the country, thanks to the Red-Hot Dress concert. No pun intended about your being 'hot.'"

"Ha... Ha..." I respond with no enthusiasm.

"I and the committee have come up with a brilliant plan."

"What plan?"

"We would like to have a fundraiser called, 'The Red-Hot Dress Arts Festival.' Because of the positive energy and money the symphony has raised, we can capitalize on this and raise money for the Boston Arts Council."

"What do you need me for?"

"Why, you'd be the mascot for our fundraising efforts."

"Mascot?"

"Yes, the official standard-bearer for the arts in Boston. Of course, you'd have to wear your Red-Hot Dress at all fundraisers and events—especially when the media is present."

"Palmer, you're off your rocker. I did it as a favor for the Boston Symphonic and to make you look bad. Why would I want to do this again?"

"Because you'd be able to increase awareness of the arts. Your celebrity is worth exploiting."

"Palmer, I don't want to be exploited. I want nothing to do with you. You're a disgusting scum bag. I appreciate The Boston Arts Council; they've done fantastic things for the Boston arts community until they miraculously installed you as its president. Since they installed you, the council has done nothing except for promoting Grandstone Galleries. I feel sorry for The Boston Arts Council, with you as its president."

"But Carla, stop…."

"Shut up. How dare you ask me for help, when you have been harassing me ever since Alexandria Savich dumped you. You turned your attention to me, asked me out on a date from hell, and vomited all over me after stuffing yourself at Legit Sea Foods with the food you ordered for you and me when all I wanted was a bowl of soup."

"But Carla, stop…."

"Shut up. You disgust me. You're an overly privileged white male chauvinist pig, with a weirdly contrived accent, slowly destroying your father's art store with your adolescent narcissistic pandering to your precious profits."

I start to hang up when I hear giggling in the background.

"Carla, you're on speakerphone. I tried to tell you, but the entire Boston Arts Council eagerly awaits your response to my proposal."

I hear a room full of enthusiastic voices, "Hi Carla, we love you," they all say while laughing hysterically.

I'm mortified. Many of the arts council members are ardent supporters of the Boston Symphonic.

I gather my composure and say, "This is typical behavior of your president. He didn't tell me we were on speakerphone. I have a proposal. I'll consider helping with The Boston Arts Council if you fire Palmer Grandstone. He's an embarrassment to the arts community with his dying art store charging exorbitant commissions for struggling artists."

I hang up the phone.

One week later, I open a letter in the mail from The Boston Arts Council.

It reads, "Dear Carla Furbee, thank you for giving us the reason and opportunity to fire Palmer Grandstone from the prestigious position as President of The Boston Arts Council. The board of directors and the council have unanimously voted to nominate you as its new president. Please let us know, as soon as you can, if you would represent us. Signed… The Boston Arts Council." There were about twenty-five signatures.

P.S. You don't have to wear your Red-Hot Dress.

27. Claire's Birthday Surprise

It's my birthday today. My mother wants me to wear this dress she bought from Nordstrom. They want me to dine with them at the Exclusive River Country Club. God, this dress is pretty. A short flowy floral dress with new cute matching designer flats. All of their rich and stuck-up friends will be there. Fancy food, chandeliers, and bow ties—yuck. Mom's so demanding and insistent that we do this. It's so annoying. I must be a good girl and go to dinner with them. I love this dress.

As I apply my smelly nail polish, my phone rings, "Claire, this is Jay Fowler. How are you doing?"

"I'm fine, Jay. I haven't heard from you since you saved me at the homecoming party from those creepy friends of Fred's."

"Creepy friends for sure," Jay replies.

I put the speakerphone on to continue with my nails, "I'd love to catch up with you and ask you how you're doing, but it's a bad time. I'm getting ready for my birthday dinner at the Exclusive River Country Club."

"Claire, you need to know something important."

"Look, Jay, I'm getting ready and…."

"Hear me out, Claire. It would help if you heard this now. I'd rather tell you this in person, but I'll do it over the phone if necessary. I was there on the day that Theo slipped on the ice and injured his hand. Fred was mad at how Theo talked back to him and how the students repeatedly chanted, 'Theo for president,' and, 'Theo Rocks.' I saw Fred slink into the bushes, knowing that Theo would soon leave the building. He stuck his foot out in front of Theo to make him trip on the stairs and slunk back to the group as if nothing had happened."

I'm in shock to hear this. I didn't know what to think or say. I'm stunned.

"Claire? Are you there?"

"So, Theo didn't just slip on the ice?" I ask incredulously.

"I saw the whole sickening incident. I was on the other side of the stairs waiting for my ride. Fred Freemark is the only person in the school who can afford custom Air Jordans. It was his right shoe that appeared from the bushes. He doesn't know that I saw the whole thing. I even took pictures of Fred's Air Jordan poking out of the bushes and another picture of Fred tripping Theo. I'll send you the pictures. Fred did it to him on purpose. He wanted to hurt Theo. He assaulted Theo."

"Seriously, he endangered me too!"

Jay replies, "The unexpected benefit of this was more significant for Fred than he ever could have imagined. He became senior class president, and they have set you up as his prized possession. Fred wants you not because of the person you are, but because of his nemesis, Theo Hall, who he thinks was your boyfriend. He hated Theo for being more popular than him and being nominated for senior class president without even running for the position. He put Theo out of the running, now he's after you to claim as his possession and to put a final nail in Theo's coffin. Fred will call and brag about how hot you are, and I'm not sure how much of this is true, but he brags about what happens in bed with you as well."

I blurt out, "I have done nothing in bed with him! I haven't even gone on a date with him."

"That's not what he's telling us."

"Liar. I could kill him!"

"He brags about how your parents and his are Exclusive River Country Club members and are in the same social circles. He's a sickening person—pure and simple."

On my phone, Jay sent me two pictures; one is a picture of Fred's leg, with his Air Jordan on, poking out from the bushes, resting on the porch, directly in front of Theo and me as we walk out of the building. The second picture is of Theo and me sliding down the stairs.

Jay says, "As you can see, Theo's foot hit Fred's right Air Jordan."

"Why did you wait so long to tell me this?"

"Well, I'm not proud of myself, and was so caught up in being in the good graces of the senior class president and captain of the football team that I kept it to myself. I hate myself for staying quiet for such a long time and apologize for not saying anything. I'm ashamed of myself, and better than this."

I just sat there in silence and was suspicious that Theo didn't slip all on his own but put little thought into it; this revelation hit me like a bombshell.

"Claire? Are you still there?"

"I sure am, Jay. When I think about it, Fred has nothing nice to say about Theo; he puts Theo down at every juncture. He makes fun of him as a wimp because of a 'boo-boo' on his hand and calls him, 'Fiddlehead.'"

"Claire, now and then, he tries to contact me, but I can't stand looking at him or the sound of his voice. He's a talented football player, and I respect him for this. We even won the state championship this year, but I have no respect for him after what he did to Theo."

"Again, why are you telling me this now?"

There was a pause.

"I was seriously thinking of hanging myself from my silence."

Jay chokes up and stutters, "I… I… needed to talk to someone. The only minister I knew of was Dr. Dawson. He taught a class at Lake Oswego High School on how the Bible has shaped history. I loved the class and thought that Dr. Dawson was someone I could talk to. I made an appointment with him. He encouraged me to tell you everything. He said it would be the only way I could live with myself."

"Jay, you talked to Dr. Dawson, and he saved another life—yours. I love him. He's Theo's minister. His wife, Alexandria Savich, is Theo's violin teacher."

"Wow," says Jay. "Dr. Dawson didn't let any of this on. I didn't even know he was so close to Theo, let alone his wife being Theo's violin teacher. He helped me out with no judgment at all. You'll have Dr. Dawson to thank for this confession. He didn't peep a word of this to anyone. He left it totally up to me."

"Thanks for the information, Jay. I believe you."

"I'm glad I could talk to you. I've always admired you. You're a stellar actress, and I especially think Theo's unbelievable. Don't let Theo slip out of your hands. Do you know what Theo's doing now?"

I respond, "It's a long story, Jay. I'm not at liberty to talk about it now."

"Claire, listen to me. If he's suffering, he needs you. You're his soulmate."

"Jay, your phone call was the best thing that could have happened to me today—as painful as it is. I'll keep you informed on developments." We end the call.

I want to wear my ripped jeans and the PYP sweatshirt that says "Theo Rocks" on the back, but it's against the Exclusive River Country Club dress codes. So, I'll play their game with no sneakers, no denim, dresses that must be a certain length, etcetera. I get ready and make myself look extra lovely with my ultra-pretty dress.

I call Dr. Dawson and tell him what Jay confessed to me.

"I was hoping you'd call me," Ben says. "What Fred did was a felony."

"It is?"

"It was an act intended to cause bodily harm. In Oregon, I'm required to report what Jay told me because members of the clergy are 'mandatory reporters.' Since Fred didn't report this to me directly, we would need Jeremy Smith to prove things. I was just about to call him and show him the pictures."

"Please keep me posted."

We pull up in front of the gigantic white pillars at the front entrance. The Exclusive River Country Club valet drives our car to the parking lot, as if we couldn't do it ourselves. We walk into the dining room, and there stands the Freemark family.

"Surprise!" they all proclaim with big happy fake smiles.

Fred stands there proudly wearing his salmon pink Air Jordans. I'll never know how he ever got past the dress code police. I'm utterly disgusted that I must socialize with the Freemarks. But some delicious ideas are forming in my head. Vengeance is boiling inside me like the Tiger Lady I've become.

"Excuse me," I say, and go to the lady's room and make a timely phone call.

When I return, we all sit down in the lavish dining room. Through the vast dining-room picture windows, you can see the Portland Spirit Riverboat slowly making its way up the Willamette River; passengers enjoy the scenery on this popular Portland dinner cruise.

Fred's salmon pink Air Jordans look ridiculous with his sports coat. "How did you get by the clothing police?" I ask, pointing to Fred's shoes.

Fred's father proudly chimes in, "The people here know that I'm good friends with the CEO of Nike. They made the shoes that Fred is wearing especially for him. The colors are unique and the only ones in the world."

"Such vivid colors. Why, they look just as delicate as Cinderella's glass slippers!"

Everyone laughs at my cute comment but does not know what this Tiger Lady is   up to.

Our expensive food in many courses is served. I act all pert and pretty. "This is fun," I say to myself. I can't wait to get my announcement out in the open. The entire lavishly extravagant dinner lasted about an hour and a half. They roll a designer birthday cake out. Everyone sings Happy Birthday. I blow out the candles.

Mom asks, "What's your wish?"

"You'll see," I say.

Fred stands and presents me with a gift.

"Open it," everyone eagerly says.

I open a box the same color as Fred's shoes—salmon pink. Inside is a ring box. I think, "Holy shit, dare I open this?"

I open the container, and there's a ring in it. It's not just any ring; it's Fred's gold football championship ring.

Fred proudly proclaims, "As you all know, our team won the state football championship under my leadership as the football team's captain. I thought you should have my prized possession for your birthday."

"Such a thoughtful gift," I say.

My brain is fomenting a touchdown. "This deserves a special thank you. You're all such a friendly bunch. Would you all friend me on Facebook? I want to post a picture of Fred on your pages. All your Facebook friends and the world need to see this spectacular picture of Fred. He's showing how thoughtful and kind he is. A picture is worth a thousand words."

Fred helps all the parent's "friend" people, as Facebook is more of a millennial thing, but they all have Facebook accounts. On everyone's public page, I post the picture of Fred's one-of-a-kind salmon pink Air Jordan sticking out from the bushes as we walk out of the high school with Theo headed directly for his foot. Another photo shows us flying down the stairs. I also post another picture that Jay sent, of Theo and me sliding toward an oncoming school bus.

"Wow, what a great job of photoshopping," Fred proclaims guiltily.

In a series of short bursts in a high-pitched voice, Fred says, "This... this... is... is... hilarious." He sounds like a laughing hyena.

I add, "It might be hard to Photoshop shoe polish. Theo finished polishing his black loafers that morning because he had to perform at an assembly with the High School Orchestra. I remember telling him that his shoes were flat—not shiny. This is because he didn't brush them after putting the polish on them. Look at the inside of Fred's right sneaker. I'll bet there's black shoe polish on it."

Fred licks his hand and attempts to rub the polish off; he fails miserably because Theo's shoe polish indelibly stained the expensive material on his shoe.

I ask Fred, "If you think they photoshopped the pictures, why don't you show us your right shoe?"

Fred refuses to lift his leg, like a dog, knowing punishment is imminent if he pees on the couch.

I see Detective Jeremy Smith and several police officers walk into the dining room right on time.

"We have a warrant for your arrest for the assault of Theo Hall. Take your shoes off. They're evidence."

They handcuff Fred and read him his rights as they escort him out of the room. He has to walk out on his stocking feet. I spit on Fred's ring, give a saliva-soaked ring to his mother, and walk out of the Exclusive River Country Club dining room. Luckily, Jeremy came with two cars. When they put Fred into a police SUV, handcuffed, Jeremy tells the other vehicle driver to give me a ride. Much to my relief, the driver is Belle, my self-defense BFF. She drives me to her house; I sit in a comfy chair in her living room stunned at what Fred did to us and my brilliant response.

28. Acquittal

One fine morning I wake up to see my mother shocked watching the morning news on television.

The reporter states, "Police released formerly missing nationally known Portland violin prodigy Theodore Hall from jail. Previously accused of grand theft for stealing jewelry from a downtown Portland jewelry store, Mr. Hall is now acquitted because of incontrovertible evidence proving his innocence. Mr. Hall was hiding in a tent to get away from all the unwanted publicity he garnered while performing on national television. Law enforcement charged a Mr. Dick Wolf, a known criminal with grand theft and rape charges in Texas, for this, and other crimes. After Wolf completes his prison time in Oregon, they will then return him to Texas for further prosecution and sentencing for crimes he committed there. Wolf stole jewelry valued at approximately one hundred thousand dollars by breaking into the display window of a jewelry store in downtown Portland. Surveillance cameras recorded Wolf breaking the store's glass display window with a baseball bat while wearing Hall's hoodie. Authorities thought Hall stole the jewelry because of the hoodie, but DNA evidence proves that Wolf, not Hall, was guilty of the theft. Portland police found the jewelry hidden in a drainpipe behind Hall's tent before Wolf assaulted Hall, sending him to the hospital. Clothing store workers reported Hall purchased the hoodie several weeks before the crime; stitched on the back were the words, 'Peace Through Global Domination.' The surveillance cameras recorded this, thus falsely pinning Hall with the robbery. Hall reported that someone stole his hoodie from his tent several days before Wolf assaulted him. Wolf attempted to rape a woman highly trained in self-defense; she blinded him in one eye among other injuries. Law enforcement will prosecute Wolf for breaking and entering, grand theft, assault and battery, and attempted rape upon release from the hospital. The woman's name is being withheld for privacy reasons. I'm Kyle Blanning reporting for KGW news."

My mother has no clue that the woman is me.

"So," I say to my mom, "Theo didn't do the crime you were so sure he was guilty of."

"He was still living in a tent. What was he doing living in a tent?"

"He was living in a tent to get away from people like your friend Fred Freemark, who unmercifully bullied Theo, calling him Fiddlehead. He was also shielding himself from well-meaning people who were concerned about a nationally known violin prodigy whose career your friend Fred Freemark destroyed. Don't forget mom, your friend Fred Freemark, who you want me to date, almost killed me and Theo with his foot decorated with a four thousand dollar one of a kind sneaker. In addition, how could you possibly cavort with the likes of Gerard Dickhoff, who thinks Theo's gay, because he plays the violin. Also, you just love to socialize with your stuck-up friends at the Exclusive River Country Club who stuff themselves with expensive food while others starve to death?"

My mother is strangely silent. But I didn't tell her of my plans to lay off Theo. It would give her too much pleasure.

29. Mount Scott

I'm at home, back in my room. Nothing has changed on the outside, but I'm not the same person on the inside. The notes keep flowing for Blast like an unstoppable waterfall.

I get a text message from Ben, "Theo, what are you doing tomorrow?"

"Nothing," I reply.

"I'll pick you up at noon. Wear warm clothes."

He hangs up abruptly. I suppose another life lesson is in the making.

The next day I get on his foaming, frothing monster bike, and we drive. We can't say much because of the wind and bike noise. Ben's getting much more confident as a biker, as he takes corners faster and seems more self-assured. What completely floors me is the American flag that's waving behind us. Ben drives to the east side of town again but heads in a different direction. We drive up to Willamette National Cemetery on Mt. Scott, overlooking the city.

We stop at the visitor center.

Ben asks me, "Have you been here before?"

"No, never. This is a beautiful place."

Ben schools me, "We're now on top of another extinct volcano, Mt. Scott—like Mt. Tabor. They established Willamette National Cemetery in 1949. In every grave here is a Veteran."

"Why did you bring me here? Did you try to make out with girls here too?"

"No," laughed Ben. "You'll see in a moment."

I hear other motorcycles arrive. Some of them are flying Patriot Guard Rider flags. Several PGRs look familiar, as they have made Lake Oswego Progressive Church their place to hang out on Sunday mornings. One by one, more and more PGRs arrive. I'd say there were about forty bikers all lined up. The leader waves for all of us to follow him. We line up on one road in the cemetery. Everyone turns off their engines.

"What are we doing here?" I ask Ben.

"You'll see," answers Ben.

No one's talking. All the bikers have this serious and focused look on their faces. The silence is like a silent prayer. I could hear birds chirping and the wind blowing in the evergreen trees. We sit here for about a half-hour while other bikers arrive.

The leader raises his hand. All the bikes start their engines at the same time. A deafening roar breaks the silence. We follow the leader down to a covered enclosure and park all the bikes perpendicular to the curb. We all walk toward the enclosure and line up silently. Many riders have big American flags with poles resting in leather flag holders. Outside the enclosure, the flag holders and the other Patriot Guard Riders stand at attention. Inside the enclosure, there's an empty altar with about ten people standing.

I recognize the chaplain who talked to me when Henry Doyle died at the VA. He smiles at me and suggests I stand with the ten people inside. Ben stays outside with the PGRs. Five well-polished active-duty soldiers march into the structure. One is carrying an urn; she places it on the altar. They all stand at attention and salute. Several rifles shoot three volleys in the air: bam… bam… bam… A military musician in uniform plays taps, on his trumpet, with perfect intonation and vibrato that wavers majestically on the last note and fades into the wind. After taps, their hands go down smartly from their salutes. They march out of the structure.

The chaplain begins, "We gather to honor twenty-two veterans who died with no family members known to them this month. They all died alone. One served in World War Two, several in Korea, many in Vietnam, and some in Afghanistan. Some didn't serve in a war but took the oath to defend their country against all enemies foreign and domestic."

The chaplain reads the name, rank, era, or war they took part in, and they ring a bell after they read each name. When the chaplain reads the last name, Henry Doyle, Sergeant, US Army, Viet Nam, he looks at me for a long time. He then reads the following, and everyone responds:

A Litany of Remembrance—We Remember Them
    by Rabbi Sylvan Kamens and Rabbi Jack Riemer

In the rising of the sun and in its going down, we remember them.

In the blowing of the wind and in the chill of winter, we remember them.

In the opening of buds and in the rebirth of spring, we remember them.

In the blueness of the sky and in the warmth of summer, we remember them.

In the rustling of leaves and in the beauty of autumn, we remember them.

In the beginning of the year and when it ends, we remember them.

When we are weary and in need of strength, we remember them.

When we are lost and sick at heart, we remember them.

When we have joys we yearn to share, we remember them.

So long as we live, they too shall live, for they are now a part of us, as we remember them.

For the first time since my accident, I have tears for something other than myself. These are strange emotions. I must have learned something in Tent City. The Patriot Guard Riders are the last to leave as they were the first to arrive. Ben and I say nothing until we get home.

We're parked in front of my home.

I ask, "How did you know that Henry Doyle was to be remembered?"

"Two ways, Theo; my stepfather called me and told me he met you on the tram, and the chaplain at the VA, a good friend of mine, figured out who you are."

"How did the chaplain figure out who I am?"

"He's a classical music fan and saw you on PBS American Prodigies. He knows that you and your family are members of the Lake Oswego Progressive Church of America."

"He didn't let this one on."

"He figured you had something to hide because Henry Doyle called you Bob, so he said nothing to you."

"So, your stepfather remembered my name. I told him my name, and he pretended he had forgotten it just a minute after I told him."

"My stepfather's a sly fox. He didn't get to be the most popular nightclub owner in Portland by not remembering names. My mother used to call him 'Fairly Honest John.'"

"So, Fairly Honest John tricked me into thinking that his memory was gone?"

"Yep. Fairly Honest John didn't want you to think that he would tell me he met you on the tram, as he was planning to do when you revealed to him that I am your pastor."

"So, the VA chaplain and your stepfather duped me. Isn't it ironic that we both have stepfathers?"

"That's why I like you, Theo; we have a lot in common: we both have stepfathers, and we are both stupid."

I laugh out loud.

"I can't believe that they conduct this service monthly."

Ben replies, "The number varies monthly, but the average number of veterans who die without relatives or friends is about twenty-five monthly in Portland!"

I say, "All this war stuff happened before I was born. Most of these veterans had no choice and were put in harm's way, like Henry Doyle. War can 'Blast' through our lives like a freight train. Here it comes, like it or not."

Ben asks, "Did you learn anything today, Theo?"

"What a stupid question." I reply.

30. Ashley Calls Theo

My phone rings. It's Ashley Rich.

"Hi, Ashley, what's up?"

"Theo, I just wanted to thank you for standing up for me at the prom. It's time to show my appreciation."

"It was nothing, Ashley. Anyone else would have done the same thing."

"Wrong." Ashley says. "Most people would have done nothing. You gave me confidence and opened up a whole new world of standing up for myself. Boys like Fred Freemark pushed me around a lot. In fact, I've discovered that I don't need to have a popular boyfriend to 'fit in.' Like you, I'm going to make something of myself before defining my life based on what other people think."

"What are you doing to make this happen?" I ask.

"College. Portland State University has a Pre-Occupational Therapy major. I don't know where this might take me, but I'm going to do something cool with my life—period."

"Wow," I say, "You're an inspiration."

"Theo, how are you doing with your hand injury?"

"Funny you should ask. I've been doodling around writing some music where I don't need my injured tendons to play the violin. I'm not sure where this will go, but it gives me some hope. From what you're planning, I need to think seriously about college again. I can't go around moping the rest of my life. If you can pick yourself up by the bootstraps and try something in uncharted waters, so can I."

"Theo, have you received any therapy on your hand?"

"No."

"My mother is an occupational therapist. I told her about your injury. She said that a colleague of hers is a hand therapist who does amazing work. She recommends you consider seeing her."

"I'll think about it Ashley. Not only that, but I'll also do something about it. Can you put me in touch with her?"

"Of course, I will."

"Thanks Ashley, you're a great friend."

"So are you," Ashley replies. "Let's keep in touch and keep each other informed on our progress."

"Absolutely," I enthusiastically reply.

31. Thomas, Brevard, Theo, and Claudia

I'm living at home now. To get out of my room, Thomas and I walk to Chuck's Place for a cup of coffee.

He clears his throat. "Do you have any plans now that you're on the mend?"

"I have some plans."

"Do you mind if I ask what they are?"

"I may have discovered something in Tent City that has promise."

"What?"

"I have been writing music. The blast from the freight train horn, near my tent, inspired me to write something I call "Blast." I think I'll submit this to Curtis. They already accepted me in music performance, so perhaps I can major in composition instead. They accepted me before my hand injury, so they may consider the total package."

"Give it a shot," Thomas suggests. "What do you have to lose?"

"Nothing, other than my pride."

"Also, remember Ashley Rich, the girl we brought home from the prom?"

"How could I forget her," Thomas replies.

"Her mother's an occupational therapist. She knows a hand therapist who may help with my injury."

"Go for it Theo. I'll support you one hundred percent."

"Thanks Thomas, on another note, no pun intended, I have an idea."

"What's your idea?"

"I know that you have been pushing for the Memorial Coliseum to be a giant place for homeless people with every service available in Portland in the facility—one stop fits all."

"What's your idea?"

"Emma's Wish is a stellar idea that has galvanized the city to help, if not eliminate, the homeless problem in Portland."

"What's your idea?"

"You have lamented, at the dinner table, how the city is a vast bureaucratic nightmare hindering your plan. You have even used derogatory words to describe your disgust with the contractor costs and profiteers who want to rip you off."

"What's your idea, Theo?"

"As you know, I have firsthand experience and knowledge of Tent City. I don't think the Memorial Coliseum is the right place to make all this happen. It would be a nightmare. Many people I met wouldn't live in a big, monumental building, and it would be too expensive and impossible to renovate for homeless people. Besides, where would the Rose Festival Parade start? It started there decades before I was born."

"So, what's your idea?"

"Okay, here's my idea: Think small. Think tiny modular home parks in abandoned or unused parking lots. The homes could be the size of say two tents. Small structures people can move, if needed, to another location. They'd be cheaper, and you could house more people this way. These homes could be located all over the city, rather than in one location. If Emma's Wish builds one such park, say housing twenty people, homeless people can occupy them as soon they open the park. The Memorial Coliseum would take years to retrofit for homeless people, and if it doesn't work, it could become a huge albatross. They could even have solar panels on the roofs of these tiny homes so that you wouldn't need electrical infrastructure."

Thomas sits there, concentrating on what I just said.

Finally, he says, "I am having trouble with regulatory agencies making this project a reality at the Memorial Coliseum. You're right. It is becoming a huge albatross. We've tossed this idea around on the board. I like your thinking, but will it work?"

"It's not my idea." I show Thomas the card: Brevard
Hallstrom, CEO, Hallstrom Properties. Commercial Real Estate
Developers Worldwide.

"We have an advocate on our side. It's a long story, but you
must talk to him."

The following week, we meet Mr. Hallstrom and his daughter
(Claudia), Miss Seventeen, at his corporate headquarters on the 42nd
floor of the U.S. Bancorp Tower in downtown Portland. We walk
into a waiting room where an efficient-looking woman dressed in a
business suit greets us with a smile.

"Would you like something to drink?" she asks us. "We have
just about anything you'd like."

"Coffee," Thomas and I say together.

She escorts us into a massive conference room, then brings
us some coffee. First, Claudia walks into the room. She looks nice.
Shiny brunette hair, ripped jeans, and white sneakers. She also has
this intoxicating smile on her face. I have a hard time concentrating
with her in the room.

"Thomas," I say. "This is Claudia. I met her while living in
Tent City."

Thomas looks at me with his mind spinning. He shakes her
hand, "Pleased to meet you, Claudia."

"Pleased to meet you too, Mr. Harrison. Theo saved my life."

Thomas's mind is whirling, I can tell. She explains in
embarrassing detail what happened.

Thomas looks at me, "You did this?"

I shrug my shoulders.

Somewhat speechless, all Thomas could utter was, "Sounds
like something Theo would do."

Claudia's father walks into the room. "Hi, I'm Brevard
Hallstrom." He holds out his hand for Thomas. They shake hands.

Hallstrom looks at Thomas and says, "I've been following
you for several years since you sold your company to Google and
pledged ninety percent of a billion dollars to Emma's Wish; I still
can't believe you did this. We use the computer models you designed
in our real estate business. When you sold, it saddened me as you
started Galaxy Communications the same way I started this business.
I always wanted to reach out to you, but I was too busy. I got to

know your son through Claudia in Tent City. We have him to thank for saving her life."

I cringe.

"When I discovered that Theo's your stepson, it all made sense. You must have rubbed off on him, as he's as compassionate as you."

I feel uncomfortable with all this adulation.

I say, "All I did was give her some food."

"Humble too," Hallstrom adds.

Thomas says, "Thank you for inviting us."

"I have a much more significant reason to invite you here today. I've been following you and the Emma's Wish foundation and I'm in a unique position in my real estate business to offer some help. When Theo contacted me to ask how Claudia was doing, I discovered you were his stepfather. I offered Theo my opinion, as it's my business to develop real estate properties—even for the homeless population. Since then, Theo, Claudia, and I have had several conversations about homelessness, especially regarding the unique situation we face in Portland. Several other cities have had exceptional results by building smaller modular homeless parks that get people off the street with portable toilets and garbage bins that help to mitigate the rat problem. These parks provide rehabilitation services, involve local charitable organizations, and keep the city, county, and federal regulatory agencies off your back, so you can get something done."

The conversation continues for several hours. We all go to lunch together. They want our input from the street perspective as well.

When the meeting is over, while Thomas and Brevard are talking, I ask Claudia what she plans to do now that she's off the street.

"I got accepted to Reed College, majoring in math and science, hopefully, to get into medical school. Several health care professionals in Tent City, who helped me with some medical issues, are my inspiration. I'll never forget their compassion. I want to do the same someday for homeless people."

Suddenly, Miss Seventeen, the skinny, helpless waif, is an eighteen-year-old woman headed for a life with meaning and purpose; she's an inspiration.

She looks at me with earnest blue eyes, "I have two questions that you probably won't be able to answer now, but I'll ask them anyway, and I think I already know the answers."

"Where are you headed now?"

"Maybe music school."

"I thought so," she replies.

"Do you have a girlfriend?"

"I'm not sure."

"I thought so," she replies.

She walks away with her father. Her shiny brunette hair bounces with every step. She turns around with a smile and blows me another kiss. I stand there perplexed.

32. Immigrant Transition Center

"Thomas, I have an idea."

"What's your idea, Emma?"

"I'm thrilled that Emma's wish is coming true. The night we were at the Heathman Hotel, seeing people treated like royalty and looking out the enormous picture windows at hungry, cold, homeless people, I begged you to get us out of there. You were so moved by my feelings you started Emma's wish. I was so busy thinking about astronomy that I didn't realize how big of a vision you had for the homeless in Portland. As much as knowing what's out there, beyond the Earth, is vitally important, so is taking care of things here on Earth. You're the best man on earth, next to Theo. I'm so lucky. I love you both. Last night, I woke up with an idea."

"What's your idea?"

"As you know, I became besties with Nadia Jama. You worked hard to bring the Jama family to our church by funding the small apartment next to the church and sponsoring Ethiopian refugees to Portland. Nadia's doing well in school and is applying for scholarships everywhere. She wants to major in urban studies to help immigrants like her family to have a place to live while transitioning to living in America."

"What's your idea?"

"I enjoy going to church in the place we occupy with Temple Beth Shalom. I've made many friends there. We have service on Sunday, and they have their service on Saturday. We've been sharing our spaces for a long time; first when they shared LOPCA and now when we share a space with them while we decide to rebuild our facility."

"What's your idea?"

"Currently, the building we're sharing with Temple Beth Shalom is being used daily instead of being empty half of the week.

The building is beautiful, and the expenses, etcetera, from what I've been told, could force the Jewish congregation to find a smaller facility. If our congregation wasn't there, this would certainly be the case."

"So, what's your idea? I just went through this with Theo. Is this a twin thing?"

"Perhaps it is, Thomas. Here's my idea. Let's stay in the current building with the Jewish congregation, become co-owners of the facility, and turn the property that LOPCA used into a refugee resettlement center with several apartments. This would make permanent full-time use of the building and provide more families like the Jama's transitioning into the United States on our original property."

There was a long pause while Thomas's brain whizzed. He took out some paper and a pencil and started putting down many numbers and ideas.

"Emma, you and Theo will never cease to amaze me. I need to give this idea to both congregations and see their response. I would need to do some homework about its feasibility, etcetera. The first person we need to talk to is Brevard Hallstrom, the father of Claudia Hallstrom."

"Why him?" I ask.

"He's a property developer with many resources," Thomas replies.

I ponder out loud, "Theo went on a date with Claudia. She's smart and beautiful. Of course, Claire's smart and beautiful too. Theo will have to figure out what he wants."

Thomas didn't even seem to hear what I just said. His brain was whizzing about my idea. But then he said, "Brevard may offer his services for free for such a venture. It was fortuitous that Theo met Claudia, as we wouldn't know of Brevard's resources otherwise."

Thomas picks up his phone right on the spot and calls Mr. Hallstrom. He puts his speakerphone on.

"Brevard, this is Thomas."

"Hi, Thomas, what's up?"

"Emma has a brilliant idea. She's on the speakerphone with me."

"Shoot," says Brevard.

Thomas explains the whole idea to Brevard.

I interject, "We need an office and other amenities that immigrants need—like a classroom to learn English."

Brevard says, "I recently built something like this in San Diego, California. Your church property sits on about the same landmass as the San Diego refugee resettlement center. It wouldn't be hard to use these blueprints. Give me a few weeks, and I'll have some plans that your congregation and the city would have to approve."

After they presented everything to LOPCA and the Jewish congregation, the decision was unanimous in favor. When presented to the city, it wasn't unanimous. Luckily, Natalie Schrunk's father, a disgraced former personal injury lawyer and now a member of LOPCA, came through and made a legal case for this to happen. The city had no other choice; so they launched the project. In front of news cameras and reporters, I got to cut the ribbon, and the Mayor of Lake Oswego, Ben, Thomas, and Brevard put symbolic shovels in the ground.

33. Claire Saves Mom's Ass

As usual in Portland, it's raining outside; it never stops—like postnasal drip. I walk home in the rain and enter the house from the back door. Mom's in the kitchen and doesn't know I'm home. I don't feel like arguing with her about my self-defense classes and everything else she's accusing me of. I sneak up the stairs and leave the lights off, so she doesn't know I'm home. Dad is out of town on business. After a few hours, I hear her scream! Then nothing. I peek downstairs and see my mom tied up and gagged with duct tape so she can't scream. I creep back to my bedroom and call 911. She's lying on the kitchen floor—probably in shock. They just walked right in through the unlocked door! I look out the window. The men are just taking stuff out of our house. They're hauling anything that looks expensive into their big truck. One guy comes upstairs—probably to get jewelry from the main bedroom. I must think fast. They could harm mom before the police get here if they haven't already done so. I grab a heavy brass table lamp and hide in the main bedroom closet. I peek from the closet door and see the stupid asshole going through my mom's dresser and putting her jewelry into a bag. While he can't stop staring at all my mom's jewelry jackpot, I quietly sneak out of the closet with the heavy lamp and hit him on the back of the head with all my might. He crashes to the floor. I yank a rope from the blinds. I tie his hands behind his back and tie his feet together before he wakes up.

I quietly sneak down the staircase. Mom's white-faced and traumatized. Belle has taught me not just hand-to-hand combat but how to think and stay calm. Mom sees me. I look at her and put my index finger to my mouth for her to keep quiet. I find the meat-pounding mallet in the drawer, take the broom from the closet, and wait by the door. As the guy walks through the door, I trip him with the broom handle. He falls face-first on the floor. I take the meat-pounding mallet and hit him on the back of the head as I did to his partner upstairs with the heavy lamp. He's out cold too. I take a knife, cut the ropes from the blinds, and tie his hands and legs up. I have rope burns from upstairs, as I had to pull the damn ropes off the blinds until they broke off.

As I finish tying him up, the police walk in with guns drawn. They came silently, not to scare the robbers. I walk over to my mom and untie her. I tell the one cop to stay with this guy. To get the other guy, I ask the other cop to come upstairs.

The cop puts real handcuffs on the guy and, after he comes to, walks him down the stairs; they put real handcuffs on the guy in the kitchen too. Since they came in two police cars, they put one in each car and lock them in the back seats.

One cop comes back in and asks us questions. "Did you subdue these guys?"

"Of course, I did. It's just my mom and me here. They had Mom tied up the whole time."

Mom says, as she's shaking, "They saw me, grabbed me, tied me up, and threw me on the floor. They threatened to kill me!"

The cop asks, "How did they not know someone else was in the house?"

"Easy," I say, "They must have been stalking the house for days and knew my father was out of town. I walked through the trails and came in the back door. They didn't see a car or me. They must have thought that my mom was alone."

Mom sits there silently.

"Well, young lady, you saved your mom from potential harm and caught the robbers. How did you have the smarts to do what you did?"

"Have you heard of Belle Brown?" I ask.

"Of course, we all have taken self-defense and offense lessons from her. She has saved our asses countless times with her knowledge and wisdom."

"I've been taking self-defense lessons from her too. She not only teaches self-defense but teaches how to think and how to use any means possible to stop assailants by using anything you can find as a weapon. I used a heavy brass table lamp, curtain rope, a broom handle, and a meat mallet against them. I didn't even need my tiger claw."

"Whoa… What's a tiger claw?" my scared shitless white-faced mom asks.

"If you're willing to talk to me like an adult, I'll tell you what it is; otherwise, you shouldn't know. Perhaps now you'll stop criticizing me and understand why I've spent so much time in self-defense training."

My Mom's strangely quiet, still white-faced, her mouth and eyes wide open.

"You should be proud of your daughter. She saved the day and possibly your life."

The cop looks at me, "I'll tell Belle what you did. She'll be proud of you."

The cops left. Later, a crew from the police department came, put our stuff back in the house, and took the robber's truck.

34. My Precious Is Innocent

The Courtroom:

"The jury unanimously finds that Fredric Phineas Freemark committed Assault in the second degree—a Class B felony. By tripping Theodore Hall intentionally, he knowingly and recklessly caused physical injury to Mr. Hall, risking Mr. Hall's life and the life of Ms. Claire Devine, who Mr. Hall was escorting down icy stairs. They both slid toward an oncoming school bus. Mr. Hall stopped the sliding by putting his hand in a sewer grate, damaging the hand that this nationally known prodigy used to play the violin. He held on to Ms. Devine and saved her from sliding into the oncoming school bus. Sentencing will take place one month from now."

"But my precious is innocent!"

"Mrs. Freemark, your outbursts at this trial are disruptive. The jury's decision is final at the sound of my gavel." BAM.

"You'll pay, I tell you, you'll pay!"

"Bailiff, subdue Mrs. Freemark."

A Rainy day in Dunthorpe:

"Must we have a tarp on the pool all year round?"

"Honey, it's cold outside, and leaves are falling. Without a tarp, leaves would fill the pool."

"Just hire someone to keep the pool clean and warm. Why can't we have it this way like the pools in Hawaii?"

"This is Portland, sweetheart, and things are different here."

"I know they're different here in liberal Portland. It's all over the news. I'll never be able to show my face again if justice does not prevail. Theo's the criminal. He was homeless, romping around with queers and drug addicts. Why, Pastor Dickhoff thinks Theo Hall is a perverted homosexual. He didn't trip on Freddy's foot. He slipped on the ice and blamed my precious for tripping him."

"Honey, you don't need to cry. You must accept the verdict. The evidence is clear. Freddy assaulted Theo."

"I don't believe it. My precious would never do such a thing. It's a hoax. Everything is a fake—fake photos, fake shoe polish, fake everything. Theo's stepfather's a billionaire who can do whatever he wants with his money. Why, he probably has more money than we do. Theo's just a homeless, immoral slob; he stole the jewelry. I'm certain of it. Like his stepfather, he wants to be richer than the rest of us, claiming to be a brilliant musician, when he's nothing but a hack fiddle player like Freddy describes him to be!"

"Sweetheart, Thomas Harrison has pledged ninety percent of his wealth to the Emma's Wish Foundation."

"It's a lie, I tell you. Harrison is still filthy rich and will stop at nothing to destroy our lives. Besides, why didn't his nursey-nurse wife take his name? Is she so vain that she doesn't want to accept the sacred bonds of matrimony and change her last name? She looks like a fake Victoria's Secret model claiming to be a compassionate caregiver for poor suffering Veterans. Likely story. She's a slut who married for money. Thomas Harrison didn't pledge ninety percent of his money to charity; he's probably hoarding most of it in the Cayman Islands, where most of our money is located."

The Attorney:

"Mrs. Freemark, I'm a defense attorney, not a judge or a jury."

"You need to release him from jail immediately!"

"I do not have the authority to release him from jail. The jury found him guilty at trial."

"He's innocent, I tell you; he's innocent!"

"The only possible way to keep him from going to prison would be an insanity plea. If we could prove that he was so jealous of Theo that he had no control over his actions, we may be able to get a temporary insanity plea. A successful temporary insanity plea may get him on the State of Oregon Psychiatric Review Board for sentencing at Oregon State Hospital instead of prison. This is a hospital for the criminally insane. Do you believe your son is criminally insane?"

"Of course not. Freddy's innocent. It's obvious. He was captain of the football team at Lake Oswego High School and was the senior class president. Why would he do such a thing? We raised him in Dunthorpe. We're upstanding members of the Lake Oswego Fundamentalist Church of America and members of the Exclusive River Country Club!"

"I brought all this up at trial at your instance, something I strongly recommended against, and the jury didn't buy this argument. The evidence is incontrovertible. Fred tripped Theo, possibly causing permanent damage, which has currently truncated his plans to be a concert violinist. This is a felony. Our only chance of keeping him out of prison is pleading temporary insanity at sentencing."

"All of this is a hoax, I tell you! They photoshopped the pictures and videos. My Freddy would never do such a thing. The shoe polish was fake. Claire Devine purposely embarrassed us at the country club with the fake pictures. We can't even show our faces there anymore. They should prosecute Claire Devine for defamation of character. She has destroyed our reputation."

"Hum, this is also an interesting idea. Would you like our firm to research this possibility?"

"Absolutely."

"Ms. Freemark. You have already used up your twenty-five-thousand-dollar retainer from the research we have done on your case and owe us another twenty-five thousand dollars for the trial. You owe us five thousand dollars for today's consultation. Would you like us to continue researching your idea that Claire Devine caused defamation of character at the Exclusive River Country Club for a separate lawsuit?"

"A separate lawsuit? This should be a part of what we have already paid you to do."

"No. According to your contract with our firm, you will pay us fifty thousand dollars for all we have done for you. Unfortunately, you lost, so you must pay all the attorney fees for the defense, and their witnesses, all of our fees, all of your so-called expert witnesses, and all court costs. A jury convicted Fred of Assault in the second degree, a Class B felony, which means people with this conviction usually get sentenced to a minimum of seventy months in prison and a $250,000 fine. The sentencing hearing will take place a month from now. You will need an attorney present at the sentencing hearing unless you want to accept the court order for the penalties imposed. You owe us five thousand more dollars for today's consultation, and you will have to pay us for preparing and representing Fred at sentencing—unless you hire another attorney. Attempting to prosecute Claire Devine for defamation of character would be a separate lawsuit that would not affect Fred's current charges and sentencing. Defamation of character has nothing to do with your son committing a felony."

"You won't get any more money from us, as you lost the case. You're a loser. My precious is innocent, I tell you, he's innocent! We'll get them. We'll get them. Justice will prevail. We'll get them!"

"Mrs. Freemark, everyone will receive what's owed to them—including your son's sentencing fine, or you and your husband will be in major legal jeopardy."

"Fuck you. Ha, Ha, Ha."

"One more little thing, Mrs. Freemark; this is your lucky day. The Hall's will not be proceeding with a civil lawsuit. Several law firms in the nation are courting Mr. Hall to represent him in a civil trial against Fred. According to every major news outlet covering classical music, Theodore Hall was the world's most promising young concert violinist. According to medical experts, Theodore Hall's international career as a concert violinist is likely over thanks to your 'precious' son."

35. A Date with Claudia

I'm preparing for my big gamble by applying to the Curtis composition department. I wonder how Claudia's doing.

I call her. "Hi Claudia, would you like to have coffee with me sometime? We went through a lot in Tent City, and I'd also like to hear more about your plans."

"How about lunch at a restaurant? My treat. I owe you at least a good meal after all the tuna and apples you gave me in my tent."

"Okay, Where?"

"Meet me at the Chart House on Southwest Terwilliger Blvd at noon. I can walk there from our home. Do you have wheels?"

"I sure do. I'll see you tomorrow."

Ben loans me his old red Honda Civic. He's so busy driving around on his Harley that he doesn't use his car unless it's raining. So, he wants me to drive it around, so it won't freeze up from non-use. I pull up in front of the restaurant, and a valet wants to park the car. So, I keep driving, find a parking spot, and walk to the front door. Damned if I'm going to give out tips as if money grows on trees.

I walk into the restaurant and see Claudia sitting at a table next to an enormous picture window overlooking Portland. I walk over to the table. Claudia's wearing a silky body-hugging dress. Damn, she has beautiful legs. What a stark contrast from the skinny girl with stringy hair, standing on the street meridian, begging for money. She is, in fact, strikingly beautiful. No, she's hot.

She stands up when she sees me, "Hi Theo. Thank you for calling. I meant to contact you to do what we're doing. Order whatever you want. Don't be shy. Daddy gave me his credit card and instructed me to treat you like royalty."

The first thing I order is San Pellegrino sparkling water in a frozen beer mug with a squeeze of lime—Ben's favorite. Claudia tries it and loves it so much that she orders one too. I order lobster bisque soup for the appetizer and king salmon for the main course. Claudia orders a roasted beet salad appetizer and the coconut crunchy shrimp main course. We share a key lime pie for dessert.

"Please thank your dad for this special treat. Since leaving the hospital, this is the first restaurant meal I've had; it's sheer heaven."

"He has more plans for you. I'm his only daughter, and you're the only boy he has ever approved of me dating."

"We're on a date?"

Claudia looks uncomfortable.

Now I feel like a total idiot, so I redeem myself, "If this were a date, it would be dream worthy."

Claudia blushes.

I take another spoonful of the decadently delicious key lime pie.

"May I ask why it was so bad with your mother that you had to leave home?"

"I'm embarrassed to talk about this, but here's what happened. Whenever my dad has to go out of the country, he hires a nanny to take care of me because my mom's an alcoholic, and he doesn't trust her alone with me. This time, she went on a real bender and fired the nanny. It left me alone with my mother. She was drunk all the time. I don't want to go into much more detail, but I had to get out of the house."

"Sounds awful."

"When my father came home, he found her passed out on the floor."

"Where is she now?" I ask.

"She's in a fancy rehab unit somewhere."

"When I called my dad, he left right in the middle of a meeting in Brussels, got on a private jet, came to my tent, and brought me home."

"Looks like you escaped a difficult situation thanks to your awesome father. So, you said you were planning to go to medical school?"

"Yep. I did well in high school in chemistry and math. My uncle's a neurosurgeon in California and has encouraged me to major in chemistry, biology, or math in college, which would be great prerequisites for medical school. Enough about me. I've read about you. Nationally famous violin prodigy damages wrist and has to stop playing. What does the future hold for you?"

"I think I'm going to music school and major in composition."

"How's your wrist doing? Does it still hurt?"

"I haven't even tried to play. It would be emotionally painful, but I wrote some music in the tent. The blast of the freight train horn gave me ideas. I know next to nothing about composing. I need some formal training if I'm going to make anything of it."

"Sounds like a plan. I'd love to hear what you have written so far in the tent."

"It'll be a while. It's a work in progress."

"What's your passion?" I ask.

"I'm a math nerd." Claudia says, "I love math. They accepted me to Reed College as a math major. One reason I applied to Reed was Dr. Alexandria Savich. She's a theoretical math professor who co-authored a book called God in the Numbers. It helped me survive in my tent. I devoured the book. I read it three times."

I could hardly wait to speak, so I blurted out, "Alexandria Savich is my violin teacher, and Ben Dawson is my pastor!"

"Are you serious?"

"Alex and Ben are two of the coolest people. I could introduce you to both of them sometime."

"Really?"

"Sure. So, you read God in the Numbers three times? Perhaps you could write God in the Numbers for Dummies someday so I can understand it."

"I had a lot of time in that tent. Your food fed my stomach, and God in the Numbers fed my mind and soul."

I couldn't believe it. Miss Seventeen (now eighteen) is brilliant. I hope to be good friends with her, but she looks as delicious as the food, which could cloud my mind. I give her a ride home. She lives with her father in a West Hills home that overlooks Portland. She gets out of the car and walks toward her house. Is it just me, or is she walking rather provocatively with the way her hips sway? Or do they do that naturally?

36. Genesis of Stage Fright Cosmetics

Emily calls me, "Hi Claire, I have something cool to tell you. Can you meet me at Salt and Straw now, where you can get the most decadent ice cream you could ever imagine?"

"Sure," I say.

With sadness in my heart, I walk to downtown Lake Oswego from my home in Dunthorpe and meet Emily at the ice cream parlor. I need some ice cream to drown my sorrows over Theo's new girlfriend and his "crickets" response to every single gesture of love I've had for him since we were ten.

I order Carrot Cake with Cream Cheese and Frosting ice cream, and Emily orders Chocolate Hazelnut Cupcake ice cream.

Crying like a river I lament, "Holy Toledo, this is the most unbelievable ice cream I've ever tasted."

"So, what's with the tears?" Emily asks.

"I'm done with Theo. He doesn't care for me so I don't contact him anymore, and he doesn't contact me. So, I must move on with life and accomplish something. I'm done pining away for Theo. He's toast. I'll get over it."

Wiping away my tears I ask Emily, "So, what did you want to talk about?"

"I have some good news."

"Sock it to me. There is nothing better than ice cream and good news to move on with life."

With a big smile, Emily says, "They accepted me to Reed College as a chemistry major!"

Suddenly forgetting about Theo, I respond, "Wow, that's way cool."

"My chemistry teacher recommended me for a four-year scholarship program for gifted students."

"I didn't know you were a gifted student."

"Thanks to Theo, who helped me with math and how to use 'brain power,' as he did with music, I excelled in math and science. I got a scholarship because I developed something in the lab that the chemistry teacher thought was nothing he had ever seen."

"Seriously?"

Emily looks at my nails and says, "Claire, your nails are as colorful as all these ice cream colors."

"I know. My mom insists I paint them to match the outfits she buys me."

Emily continues, with a sly look, "I've noticed that you always wear the most fabulous nail polish. How do you feel about enamel and acetone?"

"I hate them, but I need my fingernails to match my costumes when I'm on stage. If everything matches, I have less stage fright; I know it's weird, but my mother's obsession works for me."

"What do you have up your sleeve?" I ask.

"What if I were to tell you I have a solution to your dilemma and possibly for most women who hate enamel and acetone? I've experimented with inorganic pigments. For example, they use chromium oxide for greens, iron oxide for reds and oranges, and blues. I'm trying to expand the color palette."

"Wow," I say.

"My miracle nail polish will come off with a combination of essential oils instead of acetone. I've experimented with several formulations and found a winner; it smells like fruit and cinnamon and is beautifully moisturizing."

"What's in the 'benign formulation?'" I ask.

"I'm not tellin," Emily says.

"Why?"

"I showed the chemistry teacher what I did, and it freaked him out. He told me I should patent the formulation."

"How do you patent something?" I ask.

"It costs between $15,000 and $20,000 to patent something after attorney fees, etcetera."

"Show me how it all works."

We end up at Emily's house. I was stunned in her basement, where she set up a chemistry lab with beakers, burners, test tubes, and complex equipment.

"Are you kidding me? This is unreal."

Emily takes me to a table.

"What color do you like?" she says.

She showed me several primary colors. I picked the red. She opened a small vial and brushed my nails. I have never seen a red like that before. It didn't stink at all. It smelled about as strong as a plastic balloon.

"Wear it for a few weeks, see how it lasts, then I'll show you my magic nail polish remover."

Two weeks later, the polish looks as good as new. Emily and I are in her basement lab again. She dabs a cotton ball with something that smells like fruit and cinnamon. The polish comes off like magic. My nails haven't dried out at all.

"Holy cow," I say. "You need to get this patented."

"Again, the only problem I'm having is that I can only get primary colors. I need to do more research. Reed is the perfect place for me to do this; they have a research nuclear reactor that students can experiment with."

"Wow, a nuclear reactor?"

"I wouldn't need one to manufacture the colors, but at least I can understand how the elements work to make this happen without the reactor. It's hard to explain without going into scientific detail."

"I get it. I wouldn't understand your thinking because I barely got through chemistry class."

"I don't know the answers yet either. That's why it's a research reactor. You don't know the answer until you do the research."

"About a patent, I think we should talk to Megan Hall. Megan understands feminine beauty because she's a Swedish glamor queen, and Thomas is a big business brainiac and may have some answers for you."

I call Megan, "Hi Megan; this is Claire."

"Nice to hear from you, Claire. Even though I don't see you around much anymore, I still love you and am so happy to hear from you."

"Thanks, I love you too. I have something to show you that will knock your socks off. Can you meet me at Chuck's Place today at 2:00? Since Theo's at home and doesn't want me around, I don't want to get him all upset. So, this is between you and me."

"Sorry about Theo. He's got a lot on his plate, but I'm intrigued, see you then."

Emily and I have Megan try the nail polish. We talk all the time about glamor issues. I act in school plays; I'm thinking about a career in acting and need to know about this stuff.

"It's beautiful and doesn't stink," Megan exclaims. "Does it stay on, and is it easy to remove?"

Emily says, "Try it for a few weeks. Wash dishes, take care of your patients at the VA, wash your hands a hundred times a day, and see how it works. Here's a vial of the nail polish remover. Use it and see what happens."

Two weeks later, Megan is on the phone. "Where do I get this stuff? What does it cost? How come I can't find anything like this anywhere?"

"Emily's still experimenting with it." I tell her how her chemistry teacher thinks she should patent the formula, and how much it would cost to get it patented. Megan reacts how I'd hoped she would.

"I need to tell Thomas about this."

I get a call from Thomas, "Megan told me about Emily's amazing nail polish and remover. Before getting a patent, you'll need to have Emily do more research on the formulation. I have several patents that I needed to get when I owned Galaxy Communications."

"Emily wants to experiment with her compounds in the Reed College research nuclear reactor."

"I've heard about the reactor," Thomas says. "I hired several students from Reed when I owned Galaxy Communications. A Reed math graduate designed the algorithms we patented. So, if Emily can get the product exactly how she wants it, I'm certain I can help you with the patent."

"She starts Reed in the fall and will begin experimenting with the reactor and her compounds to see what she can come up with."

"I'll be here to support her when she's ready. Make sure she contacts Alexandria Savich when she's there."

I tell Emily about the call with Thomas, and she jumps up and down with glee.

"Claire, as bad as what's happening or not happening with Theo, I predict that someday we'll be a team. With your beauty and my brains, we'll overcome the odds."

37. Willow Speaks

I've been working with my hand therapist for several months, and just finished some hand exercises. She thinks I should attempt to play the violin and see what happens. The bus destroyed my violin in the accident, so I haven't been able to even try.

Mom pokes her head in the door and says, "Nita Van Pelt's at the door."

I guess I had better see her. She's awesome. I walk downstairs, and Nita has a big smile on her face. We hug each other. Nita is the music director for the entire Lake Oswego School District music program. Hundreds of kids love her—me included. She's holding an old familiar violin case. She encouraged me to play the violin in grade school. When I was too young to play the violin, I asked her if I could play in the school orchestra. She said that I would have to wait until sixth grade. She found a tiny violin that would fit me and gave it to me. Later, she gave me the best school violin when I was the correct size. A retired Oregon Symphony musician donated it to the school for gifted students to play. I named her Willow.

"Why don't you try her?" Nita asks. "No one has played Willow since you turned her in."

I pull her out of the case. I can't believe that I could play such a fine instrument in grade school and high school. She hasn't been tuned since the last time I played her.

Nita says, "When you got your violin, I put Willow aside, waiting for another prodigy to come along as the will says. But unfortunately, no student has qualified for her since you last played this beautiful violin."

I pick her up with fear and trepidation. I pushed playing the violin out of my mind for sanity's sake. My daymares are slowly subsiding, and I don't want them to return.

"Go ahead, try it," she implores. "Take a chance."

I haven't tuned her for quite some time. Nita has a tuning fork with her. She taps it. A perfect A is resonating at 440 Hertz. To match it, I tune all the strings. I adjust the chin rest. I play my warmup classical etude with tolerable but not intolerable pain. I'm not entirely out of the woods yet, but I'm finally hopeful.

Nita smiles at me and asks, "What now, kid?"

I'm at a loss for words.

38. Marty

Curtis is mind-blowing. The finest musicians in the world have gone here and are here now. Composers Samuel Barber and Leonard Bernstein, pianists Lang Lang and Yuja Wang, and violinist Hilary Hahn all attended Curtis. The performance standards here are the highest of any music conservatory worldwide. I'm working my ass off. My hand is still bothersome, but I'm slowly learning to compensate for the injury. I love music theory and composing. I can't get the sound of that freight train out of my mind. It starts with a blast of horns, not unlike the blast that shook me to my bones in Tent City—a B Major 6th chord. Blast is in three movements: Addiction, Treatment, and Recovery. I plan to dedicate this composition to every addict I met when living in Tent City.

Marty Steinfeld is my dorm mate at Curtis. He's a fantastic percussionist. For some unknown reason, he sees a psychologist. He drops out of Curtis, moves out of the dorm, and gets a job as a bus driver. I'm concerned for him.

I call him, "Marty, can I come over to see your new apartment?"

"Sure, when?"

"Now?" I ask.

He gives me his address.

"See you in a few," I say.

I drive my ancient five-hundred-dollar Volkswagen Bug to his street-level duplex. I knock on the door.

"Come in," I hear.

There's only one light on when I walk through the unlocked door into the kitchen, so the living room is mostly dark. Marty is sitting in a chair. He taught his cat to retrieve a small foam ball. He's throwing the ball, and his black cat retrieves it repeatedly. The cat can see in the dark.

"What's your cat's name?" I ask.

"Darkness," Marty replies.

"Darkness? That's an ominous name."

"That's the whole point," replies Marty.

"What's the point?"

"Life is darkness," Marty says. "There's nothing good about life. I'm bald with a wig and still can't get a date; I don't even want one. No one understands me because I am Jewish. When I played jazz drums, a good friend in our band died from a heroin overdose."

Marty hangs his head low and says, "There's nothing good about life."

I don't know what to say. When I lost the use of my hand, I felt like Marty. I still wonder if life is worth the struggle.

"Life can suck," I say.

Marty knows all about my hand injury and my time in Tent City.

I ask if I can throw the ball for Darkness to change the subject. "Sure," Marty replies.

I throw the ball for Darkness, and the weird cat runs after it and brings it back. Once, when Darkness drops the ball, it rolls under the couch.

When I get down on the floor to get the ball, Marty says, "Stop. I'll get the ball."

It's too late. When looking under the couch for the ball, I see a handgun.

I pull the gun from under the couch, look at Marty and ask, "You own a gun? Holy shit."

"I just got it recently for protection. You never know who might walk onto a bus."

"Protection? Is it legal to carry a gun as a bus driver?"

"I don't know," responds Marty.

"Is this thing loaded?"

"Hell yes. What if I get an intruder?"

"Wouldn't it be easier to lock your door? It was open when I got here." Marty says nothing. I carefully put it back under the rug with many thoughts about Marty's gun.

"Are you hungry?" I ask.

"Sort of," Marty replies.

"Is there any place to eat around here?"

"Yah, there's a diner two blocks from here. I eat there all the time."

We walk to the place and take a table. We ponder the menu. I order a hamburger and fries, and Marty orders a grilled tuna sandwich. While we're waiting for our food, Marty is fooling around with a sugar packet on the table.

Marty says, "I have a story about a guru. Would you like to hear it?"

"Sure."

Marty's full of stories. He never ceases to amaze me and others with his wit and witticisms.

"There was once a mother whose son won't stop eating sugar. He's driving her nuts. No matter what she does, he won't stop eating sugar. She takes the boy to a guru. She goes to the temple, gives an offering, and goes into the guru's office."

"What do you need?" asks the guru.

"Tell my son to stop eating sugar." The mother says.

The guru ponders this for a moment.

He says, "Come back in three days, and I'll tell your son to stop eating sugar."

Three days later, she comes back with her son.

The guru says to her son, "Stop eating sugar."

The woman looks at the guru skeptically. "Is this some joke? Why did I have to wait three days for you to tell my son to stop eating sugar?"

"It's simple," says the guru. "I had to stop eating sugar before telling your son to stop eating sugar."

"Good story," I say. "My pastor would love to hear this one. I'll pass it on to him. Surely, he could work this into a sermon about hypocrites who tell you not to do something when they're doing it themselves."

"Who's your pastor?" Marty asks.

"Dr. Ben Dawson. He's helped me out countless times. If you ever need to talk to someone about stuff, he'll listen to whatever's on your mind since you're a friend of mine."

Walking home, a guy is standing on the sidewalk, asking anyone walking by to come to a church service—like a carnival barker. So we go in for the fun of it. A big beefy guy is yelling and screaming angrily from the pulpit about how gentle Jesus was and how we should follow his example. When yelling dramatically about the virtues of being kind and gentle, he hits the pulpit with his fist so hard that it crashes to the ground, and his notes go flying. We're the only ones who laugh out loud—especially after the guru story. When we get back to his apartment, we bid farewell.

For the next week, Marty's gun, his dark apartment, his dropping out of Curtis, and his depressing outlook on life all haunt me. His apartment is on the way to the grocery store. On the way there, I decide to stop by his place. He has an old station wagon to carry his drums parked in the driveway. The front door to his apartment is wide open. I walk up to it and see that the light in the bathroom is on. I can see the eyes of Darkness, the cat, staring at me through the screen door.

Loud music is coming from the bathroom.

"Marty?" I yell, "Are you there?"

No answer. He probably couldn't hear me above the loud percussive music.

I walk into the house and peek into the bathroom. Marty's in his bathtub, fully clothed with the gun pointed at his mouth.

"Marty," I yell. "Drop the gun."

He looks at me, pulls the gun out of his mouth, and says, "Go away."

I turn the music off.

"Talk to me." I implore.

"Life sucks. I don't want to be around any longer."

"Marty," I say. "If you kill yourself, who will tell me cool stories about sugar? Who else could teach their cat to retrieve? What would happen to Darkness?"

"You would have been the lucky recipient of Darkness. I was about to email everyone before pulling the trigger."

I ask, "Can I call Dr. Dawson and tell him what just happened?"

"I guess so," Marty reluctantly says.

Ben and Marty have been on the phone now for about an hour. They hang up.

Marty says, "Ben wants you and me to go to the police station and turn in the gun. It's registered to me, so there won't be a problem. He then wants you to take me to an emergency room and wants to talk to the staff about my situation. He told me to give his phone number to the head shrink assigned to my case. We talked about some issues that have been plaguing me for a long time. I think I'll be okay, Theo. Dr. Dawson is awesome."

We do what Ben asked us to do.

39. Stage Fright Cosmetics

Ten Years Later:

"Action," barks the director. "Hi, I'm Claire Devine; I suffer from stage fright. When I use Stage Fright Cosmetics nail polish, it gives me confidence. It comes in unlimited colors. The nail polish and remover are completely non-toxic; their patented formulas smell like fruit and will leave your fingernails healthy and moist. They're vegan, gluten-free, and ten percent of the profits go to the Emma's Wish foundation to help end homelessness. Remember, Stage Fright Cosmetics will give you confidence."

"Cut," barks the director. "Camera: get a little closer to her face. Makeup: Claire's eyebrows need to be slightly redder to match her hair. We need to make her hair slightly closer to her eyes as well. Claire: smile a little more when the camera moves in and look directly into the camera lens. Adjust your hair with your hand so your nails will glisten in the studio lights."

I'm twenty-eight, hounded by the media, and can have anything I want. We're making a commercial for Stage Fright Cosmetics. Since becoming a soap opera star, Stage Fright Cosmetics has taken off.

Emily's sitting in the back with the film crew, she comes to me while the makeup artist fusses with my hair and remarks, "This is fun. I can't believe all the lights in this studio. They built a complete set that looks like a bedroom. Where did that antique makeup table come from?"

"I think they found it in one of the enormous warehouses full of movie furniture."

The set director chimes in, "They used the makeup table in 'Gilmore Girls' when Lorelai got her own hotel. We had to refinish it for this commercial."

"Why such extravagance?" Emily asks.

The advertising executive vice president of Stage Fright Cosmetics says, "It'll be worth the extra cost. It's a trivial expense compared to the return on investment. Your company is the hottest cosmetics company in the country now."

"From the top," the director commands. "Camera one, move in for the closeup. Action," he barks. The digital clapboard silently goes down.

"Hi, I'm Claire Devine; I suffer from stage fright. When I use Stage Fright Cosmetics nail polish, it gives me confidence. It comes in unlimited colors. The nail polish and remover are completely non-toxic; their patented formulas smell like fruit and will leave your fingernails healthy and moist. They're vegan, gluten-free, and ten percent of the profits go to the Emma's Wish foundation to help end homelessness. Remember, Stage Fright Cosmetics will give you confidence."

"Cut. It's a take."

"Let's go get a coffee," I say to Emily.

We walk to a coffee shop on the movie lot.

"I'll take that Colombian specialty coffee, straight, no chaser," I say.

"I'll take the same," says Emily.

"Emily, they grow, harvest, and roast this coffee on a volcanic hilltop in Columbia."

Emily takes a sip, "This is wonderful and intoxicating. You don't need any cream or sugar."

"Speaking of 'intoxicating,' how's Natalie?" I ask Emily.

"Natalie is teaching drama at Linfield. She loves it there."

"I loved it there too when I earned my bachelor's degree," I say. "If it weren't for Linfield, we wouldn't be in the situation we're in now."

"Claire, if it weren't for Theo, I never would have developed our nail polish. Theo believed in me and made me realize I could do anything if I just concentrated and learned the basics. Further, if it weren't for Dr. Dawson, I would have suffered from guilt that my mom divorced my dad for a woman."

"So, Dr. Dawson helped you cope with your parent's divorce?"

"He sure did. He helped me realize, like Theo did, that it wasn't my fault. Theo referred me to Dr. Dawson."

"I miss Theo," I say. "I wonder if I'll ever see him again."

"Claire, you will see him again. I'm sure of it."

"Not if I can help it. He's toast. He'll have to come back crawling on his knees begging for forgiveness before I will even consider talking to him again."

Claire, "I can't imagine a world without Theo and Claire together."

"Well, imagine it," I said with conviction.

But I think to myself, "Why did he have a picture of me in his stinking old canvas tent?"

"On another note," Emily says, "if it weren't for the research nuclear reactor at Reed, I wouldn't have been able to expand the color palette of our nail polish, and if it weren't for you and our business partnership, Stage Fright Cosmetics wouldn't have gotten off the ground. I created it, and with all of your talent, fame, and glamor, you promoted it to what it is today. We couldn't have afforded the patent we paid off long ago if it weren't for Thomas. Further, if it weren't for your stage fright, we wouldn't have come up with such a catchy name and slogan for our product. At first, I was worried that the name 'Stage Fright Cosmetics' would be a turnoff, but the slogan, "Stage Fright Cosmetics Give You Confidence," is wildly successful. It shows your human side. Who would think that Claire Devine would be afraid of a silly camera or two or three, thousands of adoring fans, and critics analyzing your every move?"

"When my nail polish matches my wardrobe, it fills me with confidence, and I don't care what they think."

"I'm still confused how the Tiger Lady, capable of disabling anyone who tries to mess with her, could have stage fright."

"I don't get it either, but it looks like we made some solid moves with our product and its branding, but the ten percent of our profits that go to get homeless people off the street means more than anything else we've done."

"I agree," Emily says.

I ask, "Speaking of the homeless population, did you run into Doctor Claudia Hallstrom when you were at Reed?"

"I did," Emily responds. "She hung out with Alex a lot. Claudia was a fan of Alex and Ben in her Tent City days. She read their book three times while in her tent down by Theo. She told me that if it weren't for Theo, secretly bringing her food and blankets, she wouldn't have been able to absorb Alex and Ben's book. Now she's a street doctor back in tent city."

"Theo never ceases to amaze me." I lament. "I'm not sure Theo even thinks about me though. He's all hot and heavy with Doctor Claudia Hallstrom."

"How are things going with Logan?" Emily asks.

"We seem to be miles apart on everything. I'm not sure what to do with him. I think he wants to marry me."

40. New York Philharmonic

Thanks to my hand therapist, I auditioned and won a seat in the New York Philharmonic as a violinist. Ashley Rich's encouragement to see a hand therapist paid off big time. Most musicians spend at least fifty thousand dollars on a violin that will win auditions, but the audition with the New York Philharmonic with my ten-thousand-dollar violin, was a miracle. When I finally got into the New York Philharmonic, Thomas bought me a fifty-thousand-dollar violin. I call her Tommie because Thomas gave her to me. This is a lot of money, although many musicians pay twice this amount. After the accident at school, when Fred Freemark tripped me, the school bus crushed my violin; I'll never let this happen to Tommie. There's a violin shop in Manhattan where most New York Phil musicians go to get their stringed instruments maintained. I had the violin maker fashion a case made of solid steel that could withstand a bus running over it. I paid dearly for this case. It weighs thirty pounds. I must carry it on my back, but I never want my violin to suffer the same fate as the one run over by a bus. Some musicians mock me for being so paranoid; others want one for themselves. It thrilled the violin maker to make more and more of these cases.

After a performance, I tell my stand partner, "I love Philip Glass. He's the greatest composer of our time."

"Yep," she replies.

I marvel, "I can't believe he showed up here to take a bow after this performance. He's a modern-day Tchaikovsky. His music is mesmerizing."

After the performance, I catch up with him, introduce myself, and hand him my "Blast" score. Knowing he would be at the concert; I had planned to do this.

"I saw your performance on PBS American Prodigies and heard about your hand injury. It looks like you made it into the New York Phil. How's your hand?"

"Not as good as I'd like it to be. I don't think it will ever heal completely. Luckily, my brain is okay—I hope."

"What am I holding in my hand?"

"I wrote something that I'd like you to look at."

Other people surround him. He holds on to my score.

I take the subway home to my apartment. New York City is the strangest place. You don't need a car. I can walk to the subway, zip to my exit, and walk to my apartment building. Now and then, I take the bus for a change of venue. I take the elevator to my apartment and make something to eat, but don't feel like eating, because I feel like I felt after playing Tchaikovsky's violin concerto with PYP—empty. I'm in the finest orchestra possibly in the world, but something is missing from my life. Claudia's entrenched in Portland as a street doc. helping homeless people. I wonder if her life has more meaning and purpose than mine.

I call her, "Claudia, how was your day?"

"Hi Theo, thanks for calling. How was my day? It was not a good day. The clinic I   work in, in Tent City, was non-stop. I had three patients with AIDS and several with bronchitis, tuberculosis, and pneumonia. One poor woman suffered from malnutrition, and I had several mental health cases: several more had wounds and skin infections. Almost all of them have poly-substance abuse issues. So that's how my day was. How was yours?"

"I played a performance with the New York Philharmonic of Philip Glass's work. He showed up at the concert and took a bow. I gave him my score of Blast. I love Philip Glass and his music."

"Our lives are different, Theo."

"I know. Even though I had a great time, I feel empty, like I do nothing for people—unlike you."

"I think if I had a choice, Theo, I would rather have a day like yours. You don't know what was going on medically with the homeless people we once lived near and with. We were lucky to have escaped the many medical issues most homeless people face."

"Claudia, has Emma's Wish made a dent in what's going on in Portland?"

"It sure has. Half of the people who normally would be homeless have shelter, food, and hope. The other half are still stuck in their places—many by choice. I feel somewhat cocooned. My medical group sees all the bad stuff. More clinics would be like ours if Emma's Wish weren't around. But countless others are still stuck in the quagmire of homeless hell."

"I wish I could do something more meaningful than playing cool music."

"Theo, you could use your talent to raise money for Emma's Wish. Claire's certainly doing something. I hate to admit it, but I'm addicted to Evenings of Our Lives. I see her in ads talking about her 10% contribution to Emma's Wish. She's a major donor to the project. She's using her talent to do good things. You could follow her example. I can't believe you let her go. I'm flattered that you're with me, but you were stupid to let her go. When will we see each other again?"

"Probably not until the concert season is over. We have rehearsals and concerts like there was no tomorrow. Perhaps I could take a trip to Portland this summer?"

"Our clinic is short-staffed now. We're all working like hell. If I were to vacation in New York, the other docs here would suffer, and so would homeless people."

"I don't like our situation," I say. "Jeremy Smith, the detective who solved the mystery of who burned down my church, had a great job in Portland as a detective for the Portland police. He fell in love with Alex's BFF, who lives in Boston and plays in the Boston Symphonic. They spent a fortune for years flying back and forth, but finally, Jeremy got a job with the Boston police as a detective. He and Carla live in Boston now, all snug and happy in a tiny little home close to where they both work."

"How do you know all this?"

"Alex fills me in. Jeremy keeps in touch with me too."

"I'd move to New York, Theo, but you haven't asked me to; even if you did, all I have is my father. I love him and don't want to live away from him."

I feel guilty about being in New York when the people who love me live in Portland. That empty feeling wells up in me again.

"Claudia, we have been dating for ten years; most of them have been apart, when I was at Curtis, and you were in medical school. Then I got this once-in-a-lifetime opportunity with the New York Philharmonic. No one ever leaves the New York Philharmonic for love."

"Theo, I have to go."

"Why so abruptly?"

"I'm tired of being alone and have turned down so many handsome suitors that it's pathetic. I want to be married and have a family. There, I finally said it."

"Marriage? Family?" I think to myself, "I'm kind of not ready for this."

"Claudia, I've been such a selfish ass. I need to do some self-reflection and decide."

"Theo, if it's that hard to decide to be with me, we need to take a good look at our relationship. I need to go now."

"Okay, can we talk tomorrow?" I ask.

"Maybe," Claudia answers.

I lament to myself, "God I'm so self-centered and stupid."

41. Dinner with Mr. Ambition

Sometimes thoughtful and sometimes charming, Logan puts together a 'romantic' dinner under the gazebo of a movie set and asks me to meet him there to discuss the next day's shoot. Dinner under a gazebo—how romantic and thoughtful. But when I arrive, the path is dark, and I stumble on some rocks. Logan's sitting at a table set for two with his cell phone lighting the table playing some tinny sounding Christmas carols. He hands me a glass of cheap warm champagne. Grips from the movie crew come to the table and serve smelly cod that's now cold on top of undercooked lentils. The nearly raw, unseasoned Brussels sprouts are barf worthy. Then, another grip comes out with a fancy display of cherries-jubilee dripping with brandy lit on fire and poured from a thousand-dollar bottle; it isn't expensive brandy in the bottle; it tastes like cheap vodka or gasoline. The ice cream has melted into a pool of watery milk. Logan's been wooing me for years. I've resisted him at every turn, but he's wearing me down. Sometimes these surprises are cute. Did he purposely make it this bad so we could have a good laugh mocking the sometimes-stupid movie scripts, or is he just being cheap? I wonder if he's paying the grips overtime.

"Claire, the entire meal and even the flowers are organic!"

"How thoughtful," I say.

"Likely story," I think.

Logan's phone goes off.

"Excuse me; I must take this call." He gets up and walks away from the table.

The entire movie crew appears from nowhere when he's on the phone. He must have given them the green light to show up on cue with cameras at the ready.

Logan returns, gets down on one knee, looks at his movie crew, and asks the camera, "Will you marry me?"

Saying no would present a firestorm of issues with the movie crew; saying yes would make everybody happy, so they could clap and get on with producing our successful soap.

After the forced situation pressures me to say yes, the crowd claps like they do in the movies.

When the crowd leaves and we're alone, Logan says, "Claire, do you realize how much it would mean for me to be an executive producer rather than a director? The sky would be the limit. I would have everyone working for me. I would have to make some risky investments with our money, but it would be worth the gamble."

"Logan, I make most of the money now. I get paid more than you do, and you'd be risking the money I make on your executive producer fantasy."

"Look Claire, you wouldn't be the star you are today if it weren't for me. I saw you acting in a musical on YouTube at Linfield. I took you to the top. Why, we could leave this silly soap opera."

I think to myself, "Perhaps the money I've made on this 'silly soap opera' is in his mind trivial, but I'm a celebrity now, and essential to the show's success; Logan is expendable, because directors are a dime a dozen. I have many fans who want to see me on television. I hope I'm wrong about his possible ulterior motives, but I'm not worried; engagements can be broken. Everyone's happy for now. Logan is usually a good guy, sometimes funny, but sometimes a selfish ass. No one's perfect. I'm already having regrets about saying yes to Logan's proposal, but they say that marriage is a lot like real estate; you get about eighty-five percent of what you want—like Jingle Bells only without dashing through the snow or a one-horse open sleigh.

42. Movie Set

We're in the coffee shop with all the movie paraphernalia: lights, microphones, cameras, and a huge movie crew. I'm behind the counter, acting like I'm making coffee and selling cupcakes.

The makeup artist fools with my hair right before the First Assistant Director calls, "Action."

Six-foot-three movie stud Brooks Rich (a nice sensitive gay guy in real life) walks in the shop with his big black eyelashes and neatly coiffed hair all dyed jet black. Wardrobe gave him a thick, expensive-looking overcoat with a matching scarf draped around his neck. The cameras roll backward on a track as he walks in. He stops at the counter and looks at me earnestly.

End of scene.

Next scene:

"Action."

Brooks: "Are you sure you want to stay in this little hick town?"

Scarlett: "I want to stay here. I hate my job in the city. I fell in love with the people and want to stay here and make a life here. My father's Christmas tree farm and my sister's cupcake shop are the most important things in my life right now."

Brooks: "I know you love this place, I do too, but you could make millions if you'd convince your father to sell his Christmas tree farm to my company to build condos."

Scarlett: "I resigned from my corporate job in the big city and will live here permanently."

Brooks: "You're making a big mistake, Scarlett."

End of scene.

Next scene:

Brooks walks out of the shop in a huff with cameras following him on the same track.

We get ready to shoot the next scene. The movie crew doesn't want to change anything, including my hair, makeup, wardrobe, lighting, sound, etcetera, because Joey will be in it. They already filmed him pulling up in his old red pickup truck yesterday, but they'll cut this scene right before the scene we're about to shoot. We never shoot a movie sequentially. We could shoot the first scene last and the last scene first. It all depends on how much time and money it takes to move cameras and equipment.

Joey walks into the shop and comes up to the counter. I'm still acting like I work here.

Joey: "Brooks didn't look so happy when he got into his car. I didn't know the wheels could squeal when taking off in a Mercedes."

Scarlett: "I just told him I'll be staying here, and the farm is not for sale."

Joey: "You'll be staying here, in Hartsville? What about your corporate job in Boston?"

Scarlett: "I quit it. Joey, we grew up together in this town. I never noticed you until you invited me to the senior prom, and I turned you down."

Joey: "I know. I remember that day well."

Scarlett: "If you invited me to the senior prom today, I would say yes. You've done more to protect the values of my hometown than anyone—you and your famous red pickup truck."

Joey: "I'm just being myself."

The cameras move in. We're in focus, but the background behind us is out of focus with the movie industry's romantic bokeh effect. For a long time, we stare into each other's eyes, but to keep the series going, we can't end this with a kiss, or we wouldn't be able to continue the story.

The director yells, "Cut. Magnificent scene."

Earlier, we had filmed a scene where someone runs into the coffee shop yelling, "The Christmas tree farm, the Christmas tree farm, is on fire!"

And so, the series continues with a crisis that keeps Joey and me from kissing. As the storyline goes, the mayor, who wants the town to be developed under Brook's company, wants to blame Joey for the fire. Does this miscarriage of justice keep us apart or make our love grow stronger? The faithful Evenings of Our Lives viewers know who started the fire but must watch the next episode to see if good will triumph over evil.

43. Darcelle's

"Natalie, I have a surprise for you."

"Emily, what do you have up your sleeve now?"

"Ever since we've been together, Natalie, it's been all work and no play. I've been all consumed with Stage Fright Cosmetics, and you've been busy teaching drama at Linfield. We need a break from all work and no play. Put on your blindfold, and we're going on a car ride."

I drive downtown to the designated spot and find a parking space. Natalie's still blindfolded as I walk her to the entrance.

"Watch your step; there's a curb in front of you."

We can hear music at the entrance. We walk in, and I take Natalie's blindfold off.

Natalie yells above the music, "Is this Darcelle's?"

"It sure is," I yell back.

"I've never been here before but have heard so much about it."

Sparkly dresses and capes. Men in six-inch heels. Wild hair. Tons of makeup. Inch long eyelashes. A lighted life-sized outline of a martini glass with a flashing olive behind the stage. Big green hair. Wild big hairdos. Pride Northwest.

We absorb the ambiance for a spell and order some drinks. Then, I couldn't believe my eyes.

"Emily, do you see what I see?"

"What?"

"Behind that yellow cape and frizzy wild hair with fake eyelashes and gobs of makeup is Pastor Gerard Dickhoff! This guy left my father for dead ten years ago when they got into a car accident together."

"He just left your father in the car? Was he unconscious?"

"Yes. Dickhoff didn't want to be caught drunk at the scene of an accident with my father, so he left my father unconscious in the car. Two guys rescued my father, and he's alive today. He left Pastor Dickhoff's church and is now a proud and sober member of the Lake Oswego Progressive Church of America."

"How did Dickhoff not end up in prison if he left the scene of an accident?"

"My father pretended that there was a camera on his car that showed him running away. Dickhoff believed him and turned himself in, a lesser crime than lying about it and being seen on camera running away."

Emily says, "I remember him well when the Lake Oswego High School LGBTQ Alliance went to his so-called church, and we made a divine scene. He accused us of many grave abominations against God. Look at him now; he's dancing, flinging his wild frizzy cape, and flirting with the other cross-dressing men."

"He doesn't know what you look like, Emily. Get some pictures of him."

Lake Oswego Review headline one week later:
"Pastor Dickhoff Sparkles at Darcelle's."

The article reads: "Gerard Dickhoff pictured here at Darcelle's, is enjoying himself dressed up as a female. Dickhoff is the pastor of the Lake Oswego Fundamentalist Church of America. They formerly convicted him of leaving the scene of an accident with a severely injured driver who would have died had passersby not rescued him. He wiggled out of legal jeopardy by turning himself in and is now the pastor at FUCA. Gerard Dickhoff runs a gay conversion program there."

"When asked about his appearance, dressed up as a woman, Dickhoff stated he was undercover researching the perverted gay lifestyle for his gay conversion program. When confronted with the fact that dressing up as a different gender has long been part of English leisure culture, enjoyed by many people of all sexualities, Dickhoff stated, 'Everyone who's not a normal heterosexual is perverted and needs to be converted.'"

The pastor then said with great conviction, "The Bible clearly states what should happen to perverts and deviants."

He opened an old worn King James Bible and read from a list in it.

Kill adulterers, Leviticus 20:10
Kill all witches, Exodus 22:18
Kill anyone who sins, Ezekiel 18:4
Kill the curious, 1 Samuel 6:19-20
Kill gays, Leviticus 20:13 and Romans 1:21-32
Kill men who have sex with other men, Leviticus 20:13
Kill any bride discovered not a virgin, Deuteronomy 22:21

"When asked why he's converting gays when his Bible says to kill them, he said, 'God almighty has given me special powers to interpret the Bible in ways that will benefit my flock and mankind in general. When I convert sinners, who become repentant heterosexual men, they don't have to be killed.'"

"Should we kill or convert women too?"

"You're trying to trick me, and I resent this! Here is the bottom line for all of you new-age hippy millennials. Any sex at all, unless intended for procreation by a man and a woman, is an abomination in the bonds of holy Christian matrimony."

The pastor stormed out of the room.

When we questioned FUCA officials about Gerard Dickhoff cross-dressing at Darcelle's, they issued the following statement, "Pastor Dickhoff is the irreplaceable and invaluable leader of our congregation. We believe that whatever Pastor Dickhoff does is the will of Father God Lord Jesus Christ as Pastor Dickhoff's wisdom benefits our church and mankind. We're certain that he was researching the perverted gay lifestyle as he states."

"When asked how much money they generate from FUCA's gay conversion program, they refused to answer."

44. I Want to Be Like Theo

"Dad, why do I have your name and not mom's?"

"It was your mom's decision. People would call her Alex Savage when she was in school because it rhymes with Savich. She didn't want this to happen to you."

"But mom plays the violin like a savage. She's so good that it freaks me out. I want a new violin."

Alex butts in, "It won't be that long before we can get you a full-sized violin. You must grow a few inches before we can get you one."

"But my violin doesn't sound as good as your violin."

"It can't sound as good as mine, honey. Gennaro Gagliano made my violin in Naples, Italy, in 1755. It costs well over $250,000. We'll get you a fine violin when you're a few inches taller."

"Mom, do you teach math and play the violin at the same time?"

"No, but music and math have a lot in common."

Now I butt in, "Your mom has many talents. Currently, she's teaching theoretical mathematics at Reed College. She's on the verge of publishing another book and plays in Chamber Music Northwest. She had a full-time career as a concert violinist and a recording artist. Paradoxically, she's a complex woman who can do more than one thing well. You're the lucky recipient of her genes and have the best violin teacher on the West Coast as your math tutor."

"Mom, you were Theo Hall's violin teacher. He's a legend in school. My orchestra teacher thinks he's way cool."

"What did she say about him?" I ask. "she said he was a violin prodigy headed for international fame until he slipped on the ice and destroyed his left arm, but also said that he made a big turnaround and is now in the New York Philharmonic! Is it hard to get into the New York Philharmonic?"

"It's nearly impossible to get into the New York Philharmonic, sweetheart. You must be one of the top musicians in the world to get a position in the New York Philharmonic."

"Mom, Dad, I want to be like Theo."

45. Marty's Comeback

I get a text from Marty. "What's happening, man? I heard you're in the New York Philharmonic. How cool. I'm in New York for a few days. Do you want to meet up?"

I text back, "Sure."

We're in a coffee shop near my apartment. Marty's still bald, has a healthy-looking beard, and is wearing a baseball cap.

"Marty, what have you been up to for the last decade?"

"I still live in Philly. So, I returned to Curtis, graduated, and landed a position playing the timpani with the Philadelphia Philharmonic."

"That's fantastic," I say. "When I reached out to you, you said you were doing fine and wouldn't tell me much more. Then, you never got back to me."

"I had a lot of issues to deal with and needed some time to sort things out."

"If you don't mind my asking, what were your issues?"

"As you know, I dropped out of Curtis and got a job as a bus driver. As a result, my parents insisted I see a psychologist. But unfortunately, all the psychologist did was prescribe antidepressants. As a result, I gained weight and became even more depressed. I didn't want to live."

"Well, I'm glad you're still around."

"After you saved my life, Dr. Dawson helped me to realize that I'm gay; it tormented me for years. When you connected me with him, he worked with the psychology team at the hospital and convinced them not to give me more antidepressants. Being a closeted gay man was the major cause of my depression. I didn't need anti-depressants; I needed a community that would openly affirm me just as I am. So I connected with a Progressive Church of America in Philly and now have an open and affirming family."

"Sounds like something Ben would do," I say.

"He figured out what was bugging me on that first phone call the day you found me in my bathtub. After that, we had many calls for almost a year. He spent a lot of time talking to me. I asked him about this, and he said, 'Any friend of Theo's is a friend of mine.'"

"I told him you saved my life. Do you know what he said?"

"No."

"He said, 'Sounds like something Theo would do.'"

"All I did was show up at the right time."

"Theo, you did a lot more than that. You were a perfect friend. How precious is that? You also connected me with Dr. Dawson."

"I guess so," I say.

"Enough about me," Marty says. "What's happening with you and the famous movie actress Claire Devine? You told me about her while you were dating Claudia Hallstrom. Are you still with either of them?"

"It's a long story, Marty. For the last ten years, I've been in a long-distance relationship with Claudia. I was in Philadelphia at Curtis, and now I'm in New York City, while she has been in Portland the whole time. I only see her when I visit my family in Portland. She wants more than I do out of the relationship. I'm only twenty-eight, and don't feel right about continuing with her when she wants to take our relationship to the next level, and I don't. I don't know what to do. She's pursuing her dreams as a street doctor in a mobile clinic in Portland, helping homeless people with their unique medical issues. She's beautiful, her daddy's rich, but I don't think I'm in love enough to spend the rest of my life with her."

"What about Claire? You said she was your girlfriend ever since you can remember. What happened?"

"The relationship with Claire just ended. She pulled away, and I've been wrapped up with Claudia ever since."

"Theo, are you in love with Claudia?"

"Sort of—I guess."

"What do you mean, 'sort of?' Let me get this straight. You just let Claire Devine go? God, you're stupid, but in other ways you're smarter than the rest of us. I'm gay but totally in love with Claire Devine. She's not just any soap opera star. She… she's awesome, and human at the same time. You have a problem, Theo. I met Claudia a few times when we were at Curtis. She's nice, smart, and successful, but I just don't see you two together forever. Claire's the most spectacular actress on television. My partner and I are Evenings of Our Lives addicts. She's in our home every day."

"You're a soap opera addict?"

"I'm not a soap opera addict. Steve and I are Claire Devine addicts. She's captivating, smart, compassionate, beautiful, sexy, and spectacular, and you just let her go?"

"You're right," I say. "Dr. Dawson once explained how stupid he was when he was my age. I think he was trying to tell me something. He never mentioned Claire, but he can see things most people can't. I kind of miss Claire. In fact, Something's missing in my life—Claire's missing."

"Theo, you need to talk to Claire before she ties the knot with someone else!"

"Marty, I believe you're right. I'll keep you posted."

46. Blast Debut

I answer my phone call from an unknown number. "Theo Hall," I say.

"Theo Hall, this is Philip Glass."

I just sit there in silent shock. I'm on the phone with my idol.

"Hello? Are you there?"

"I'm here."

"Holy God, Theo, your symphony is magnificent. I've contacted the New York Philharmonic and asked them to play your work; It would thrill me to introduce your work to the public—with your permission of course."

Several months later the New York Times Music Page headline reads: "Blast Blast's the Audience into a Standing Ovation."

The article reads: "Theo Hall, a New York Philharmonic violinist, wrote a symphony that the New York Philharmonic played last night at The Lincoln Center called 'Blast.' The audience loved it. So did this reviewer. In an interview with Mr. Hall, he says that his experience living in a tent near railroad tracks in Portland, Oregon motivated him to write the piece."

"What inspired you to write the symphony?"

"I became quite familiar with the blast of a train's horn when I lived near the railroad tracks in Portland's Tent City. Horns on trains are all different. The locomotive I'm familiar with blasts its way through the neighborhood unannounced with a B Major 6th chord, the same chord that frequently occurs throughout Blast. Several times during the symphony, there's a glissando to mimic the Doppler effect when a train passes by. Some horns on the train were out of tune from years of outdoor use, and it nearly drove me insane. When I wrote Blast with some of the French horns out of tune while playing the B major 6th chord, it drove the horn section out of their minds too. But, this is what makes the symphony what it is. The piece is in three movements, Addiction, Treatment, and Recovery. During Addiction, the French horns are way out of tune while playing the chord. During Treatment, they are more in tune, and during Recovery, the horns play a perfectly in tune B major 6th chord; this is what gives the piece such a satisfying ending.

"How did you end up living next to railroad tracks in Tent City?"

"To make a long story short, after playing Tchaikovsky's Violin Concerto in D with the Portland Youth Philharmonic, and performing on PBS's American Prodigies, I thought I'd play the violin for the rest of my life, but shortly after all this happened, I had an accident that damaged my hand, and I thought I'd never play the violin again. I needed to get away from well-meaning people hounding me. I ended up in a tent near the railroad tracks."

"How were the three movements, Addiction, Treatment, and Recovery, inspired?"

"Many of the homeless people I met in Tent City were addicted to drugs. Several who sought treatment got out of Tent City permanently."

"Is it true that someone assaulted you there and accused you of stealing jewels?"

"That's correct. They found the perpetrator of the crime guilty because of DNA evidence, and they acquitted me."

The reporter responds, "From living in a tent next to a freight train to writing a major symphonic work, debuted by the New York Philharmonic, is quite an achievement."

"Thanks but were it not for my hand injury and my experience in that tent, I wouldn't have written the symphony, and wouldn't have realized that life wasn't over because of my hand injury. I must also thank my family and everyone who supported me through the ordeal. I also must thank my pastor, Dr. Ben Dawson, for telling me the story of a lima bean."

"Do you mind sharing this story?"

"I'd love to. If you push a lima bean down the side of a glass and watch it grow, the stem will grow up, and the root will grow down. If you turn the lima bean upside down where the stem is facing down and the root is facing up, the stem will make a U-turn and grow up again. The root will do a U-turn and grow down again. If you do this repeatedly, the little lima bean will do countless U-turns until it runs out of nutrients in the soil and dies. I had to act like a lima bean and make a turnaround."

"It looks like you made quite a turnaround, like a lima bean, and changed your life from a performer to a composer."

"I still play the violin but can never play like Joshua Bell, or Hilary Hahn for instance, because of my injury."

"Many people have compared your symphony to Bach, citing Bach's Toccata and Fugue in D Minor with similar chords enhancing the piece, and Philip Glass's music, which is new and mesmerizing, breaking all the rules of even contemporary classical music. Some have compared your work to Bernstein's Age of Anxiety as well. What are your thoughts on these comparisons?"

"I love Bach, though I'm not worthy of being compared to Bach. Bernstein and Glass are huge inspirations. Philip Glass was the first to see my manuscript and recommended to the music director of the New York Phil to consider playing it. He also introduced me at the concert which was the biggest honor I could ever think of."

"Thank you for sharing your thoughts. We look forward to hearing more of your outstanding work in the future."

"Thank you for interviewing me."

47. Break Up Number One

I'm in my New York City apartment. Claudia calls from Portland and says, "Theo, I'm not sure I can hang on much longer in limbo like this. You're treating me like you treated Claire. I only have a few more years left to find someone who wants a family. I'm a medical doctor now and working for a non-profit giving medical care to homeless people in Portland. My dream is coming true. My life has purpose and meaning, but I can no longer deal with this long-distance relationship."

I can't say anything. No matter what I say, it will be all over. I love her, although something is missing. What's missing is Claire; Marty's right; she's, my soulmate.

"Something is missing, Claudia. I don't want to tie the knot only to discover that a lifelong commitment may not work out for us."

We decide together to break up.

I don't enjoy walking around the city at night, but I do it anyway.

After the Tchaikovsky concert with PYP a decade ago and my big debut with Blast, I have the same feeling. I'm on a train looking out the window at a devastated landscape, and there's nothing I can do about it.

As I walk past storefronts, bars, and convenience stores, I hear music from nightclubs and the never-ending sounds of traffic. I can hear and see what's going on but feel like I'm not a part of it—like I'm in a hermetically sealed tube struggling to breathe.

The world is a wasteland without Claire. I long for her.

Because of my stupidity, as Ben pointed out, I might lose her.

I need to get off this train to nowhere and see if Claire will have me.

As I walk down Fifth Avenue, in the city that never sleeps, dawn approaches.

In my sleep deprived brain, it dawns on me that I need to make another turnaround.

48. Stalking Claire in Vermont

I Google Claire Devine, it reads, "Claire Devine is currently filming Evenings of Our Lives in Chester, Vermont."

Soap Opera News posts pictures of her, and some director dude proposing to her. Thankfully, there are no pictures of her getting married yet, so I'd better do something or lament my stupidity forever.

I leave Pennsylvania Station in New York at 11:30 A.M. and arrive at the Bellows Falls Train Station in Vermont at 5:26 P.M. I rent a car and drive to Chester and get a motel room. In the morning, I go to a coffee shop. I get my coffee and sit at a table with a newspaper on it. I'm stunned to see Claire walk in with several people, some with suits and some with long hair, jeans, and sweatshirts. It looks like the executives and crew of a movie shoot. I hide behind the newspaper. Claire's natural red hair is long and luxurious. She sits next to a handsome man with makeup on, probably her love interest in the soap. She's a movie star. I don't know what to do. It appears as if they're getting ready to film something.

I hear them say that the shoot will be at the Haverford Christmas Tree Farm later in the day. Every single fiber of my being yearns for her. So why did I lead Claudia on for so many years? Claudia's a beautiful person devoted to me like Claire was, but something was missing. So soon after my breakup with Claudia, I feel like a stalker, going after an old flame.

I drive to the Haverford Christmas Tree Farm. I see many trucks, opened from the back, with movie gear in them. Several are power supply trucks for lighting that are nearly silent as they supply power for outdoor movie lights. Massive cables follow the trail; I follow them, get off the trail, walk carefully in the snow, and hide behind a future Christmas tree.

"Action," calls the director. A digital clapboard silently goes down in front of the camera. There's a lengthy track that a cart sits on; the camera and operator are on the cart. People pull it backward as Claire, and the handsome actor that was in the coffee shop, walk down the path on this Christmas tree farm. Sound engineers hold mikes above their heads; lighting people also track them softly lighting up their faces—even in the shade. I can't hear what they're saying clearly, but from my vantage point, the dialogue is about living the corporate life in the big city or staying in this small town, where her sister started the famous cupcake shop. Should I reveal myself? If so, when? They'd probably arrest me if I jumped out from behind the trees. I slink away unnoticed.

The next day I again have breakfast at the coffee shop. They also serve real food. As I dive into my bacon-topped waffle soaked in local Vermont-made maple syrup, Claire and the crew walk in again.

She sees me.

"Claire?" I say.

"Theo?" She says.

I'm unable to eat my food. We look at each other silently, saying nothing. Claire's gang of moviemakers' wave for her to come to their table. She waves them off and sits at my table.

Acting innocent, I ask, "What are you doing here?"

"We're shooting a movie."

I had to pretend that I knew nothing about Claire.

"Wow, you're a movie actress?" I ask stupidly. I'm a terrible liar and actor. How would I not know she was an actress? She's famous. One movie maker comes to our table. I stand.

"Theo, this is Logan, my fiancé. He's the director of the movie we're working on."

"Nice to meet you, Logan. I was here by coincidence, and an old friend walks in—Claire. We haven't seen each other for ten years."

"I've heard a lot about you, Theo. Claire's mentioned you several times. In fact, you're hard to compete with, and quite an annoyance." He said this with a smirky smile on his face.

I think to myself, "She still thinks about me?"

"Theo," Claire asks, "Why are you here in Vermont?"

"I'm on a little mini vacation. I live in New York City and need a break from things."

"What things?" asks Claire.

"I'm a violinist in the New York Philharmonic." I didn't tell her about Blast.

Claire's eyes widen. "I guess you got over your injury."

"Sort of. I went to Curtis, and the rest is history. I'm not quite back to where I was because of the injury, but I'm getting there."

"You?" I ask Claire.

"I graduated from Linfield College majoring in theater arts. Logan saw me performing there on YouTube and brought me into his world of soap operas. Then Emily and I started a nail polish company, thinking it was just fun, but it has taken off."

"What's the name of the company?"

"Stage Fright Cosmetics."

"I've seen ads for this stuff." How could I not know that Claire Devine wasn't a part of the company when all the ads have her in them? I'm so bad at this.

"How did it all come about?"

"It's a long story, but Emily Young majored in chemistry at Reed, thanks to you for helping her out with her math. She fooled around with weird organic-colored substances. She devised an environmentally sustainable nail polish that will come off with an essential oil solution rather than acetone. I do the publicity, and she's the brains behind the product."

"How did you come up with the name?"

"I've always had stage fright, but when my nails match what I'm wearing, it gives me confidence—hence our slogan, 'Stage Fright Cosmetics Give You Confidence.'"

"I remember you always painted your fingernails pretty colors in the high school plays. That's a hilariously brilliant slogan and apparently highly successful."

Logan butts in, "If it weren't for me, who gave Claire her first break in the movie business, the 'hilariously brilliant' slogan would never have gotten off the ground."

Logan wants to stop this brief reunion. People wave for Claire to get back to their table.

Logan huffs, "Claire must get back to our pre-production meeting before the next shoot. If you'll excuse us."

"I'll join you in a few," she says to him.

Claire doesn't budge. Logan storms off.

Finally, I say, "I'm sorry."

"Sorry for what?" asks Claire.

"I'm sorry for my stupidity. Sorry for not realizing what we had. Sorry for being such an inconsiderate self-centered narcissist."

"I agree," she says. "You were all those things. But I was always in your face and never gave you a chance to reciprocate. So, I'm sorry for being such a nuisance."

Claire fumbles with her purse. She pulls out the picture I hung behind the flap in my Tent-City tent and hands it to me.

Stunned, I ask, "How did you get this?"

"It's a long story," Claire replies.

She writes her phone number on the back of it. "Call me," she says. "I miss you."

A tear pops out of her eye. She goes to the women's room, probably to get her composure back before joining her movie-making team.

I ask myself, "How did she get this picture? Was she in that tent looking for me!" The love of my life was right before my eyes, and I was so stupid that I dropped her just like that. Ben's right. He's just as stupid as me.

49. Claire visits Carla

Theo hasn't called me; it's been two weeks. I need to talk to Carla about this disturbing development. It's a two-and-a-half drive from Chester, Vermont to Boston, where we're shooting Evenings of Our Lives. Jeremy got a job in the Boston Police Department and isn't home now. I park my car right in front of their small home. I knock on her door.

"Hi, Carla. Thanks for seeing me today."

We hug.

"How are you and Jeremy doing?"

"We're fine. We've been in this home for five years now. But, God, it's expensive to live in a 1,075-square-foot home in this neighborhood. It takes both of our salaries to afford this humble home on Eighth Street, but it's close to our jobs, so we don't have to spend hours commuting. It's only two and a half miles to Symphony Hall for me and three and a half miles to the Boston Police Department for Jeremy. Quincy Bay is only a block away. Should we decide to have children, we may have to move into a bigger home, but for now, this will do. We're both thinking of not having children."

"Each to his or her own," I say. "Children are a gigantic gamble, and I love your home."

"So, why do you want to talk to me today?"

"Many reasons." I start counting with my index finger. "One, I love you. Two, you know about women's issues. Three, you taught me a lot about the oboe. Four, you know things about men I will never understand. Five, I ran into Theo in Vermont during a movie shoot. I'm engaged to Logan, as you know, and when I saw Theo, my heart pumped wildly, my face flushed, and I couldn't stop thinking about him. So I gave him my phone number. But unfortunately, he hasn't called me back for two weeks now."

"Was it a chance encounter?"

"I don't think so. During our morning pre-production meeting, I saw Theo in the cupcake shop hiding behind a newspaper. Later that day, I saw him sneaking around in the forest during the shoot. I nearly forgot my lines. So, I had to act like it was a chance encounter when he showed up in the cupcake shop the next day. But, of course, he pretended it was a chance encounter too."

"Sounds romantic," Carla says.

"I don't know what he's up to. Why hasn't he called me?"

"Claire, look at that big fat engagement ring on your finger. Would a gentleman like Theo get involved with an engaged woman? I suspect he's depressed about your marriage plans and does whatever he can to get you out of his mind."

"You're right," I say. "I'm not sure what to do. I still love Theo damnit, but he never lifted a finger for me. When I saw him, all the feelings I've had for him since grade school popped into my head, and I can't let them go."

Carla also starts counting with her index finger. "One, perhaps he grew up in the last ten years. Two, are you sure you want to marry Logan? Three, why do you suppose your heart started to 'pump wildly' when you saw Theo? Four, why did you come here to talk to me about him? Five, if you had no feelings for him, it would have been easy to think of him as an unwanted stalker. But you're here questioning your feelings."

She hit the nail on the head. I'm questioning my feelings for Theo and my engagement with Logan.

I ponder out loud, "Logan is all politics and little substance. He's bound and determined to make it up the movie industry success ladder. His current position is not because of talent or passion. He's not the best director I've worked with. He wooed me with this enormous ring and is probably using the installment plan to pay for it. All he can think about is money. I'm realizing that all I am, is his future bank account and arm candy. He was also rude to Theo in the coffee shop."

"Of course, he was rude," Carla says, "He's jealous of Theo, just like Fred Freemark was."

"When we were younger, I was like a stalker. I wouldn't leave Theo alone. I was so infatuated with him that I would get in his way at every turn. He would always apologize for bumping into me if I got in his way purposely at school. I guess he just got sick of me.

Now, he appears to be bumping into me purposely. It's funny, ironic, and more romantic than the silly soap opera I act in."

"Claire, did you know Theo wrote an entire symphony? It debuted with the New York Philharmonic last week."

"Seriously? He didn't mention it."

Carla shows me the New York Times article with his interview in it.

"I've been so busy that I haven't had time to read the newspaper."

As I read the article, I comment, "That sickening place they call Tent City inspired him to write an entire symphony? That's where it all happened—Theo's assault and my attempted rape. Holy cow. It's just like Theo making lemonade out of lemons. He also has the humility not to brag about his accomplishment."

"Claire, I'm not supposed to know this, but Theo broke it off recently with Claudia Hallstrom."

"He did? Tell me more," I say excitedly.

"Don't ask me where I found this out, but Theo's single and probably lonely as hell and longs for you. I'm certain several attractive symphony musicians in the New York Philharmonic are eyeing him. He's vulnerable. If you don't think seriously about your plans to marry Logan, you'll miss out on Theo."

"This is a lot to think about. Are you sure you can't reveal your sources?"

"You can put two and two together. My BFF, Alex, was his violin teacher. She lives in Portland in the same neighborhood as Theo's family. Do you get the picture I swore not to reveal? He's a hot property—cute, talented, and sensitive. He's on his way to becoming a major composer, all grown up, and isn't the same person he was in grade school."

We make some sneaky plans. But first, I must do something I should have done a long time ago.

50. Break Up Number Two

Logan and I are having dinner at Country Boy Diner in Chester. We had a long day of shooting. Since he asked me for dinner, he chose this place because it was cheap—like him. Since we sat down, he has been on his phone. He excuses himself from his phone call long enough to order and keeps talking, ignoring me, until the food arrives. He eats while talking on the phone. Finally, the call ends.

"Who was that?" I ask.

"Just important business stuff you wouldn't understand," he replies.

"Try me," I say.

"Look, Claire, you may have found some success with your cutesy nail polish company and its catchy little slogan, but the movie industry is a much more complicated animal."

"Have it your way," I say.

He orders dessert; I decline.

"Logan, we need to talk about something important."

"What?" He asks while digging into his apple pie à la mode.

His phone rings again.

"Excuse me," he says, "I need to concentrate on this phone call."

He gets up from the table and takes his call outside the diner. The conversation I had with Carla comes clearly into focus. The server comes by our table to fill up our coffee cups. I have a brilliant idea.

I look at the poor waitress, probably struggling from day to day to survive, or she wouldn't be working here.

"Are you from Chester?" I ask.

"Born and raised here."

"Do you have a family?"

"It's just my mother, me, and my two sweet little munchkins."

"Husband? If you don't mind my asking."

"Hell no. I divorced his ass when I caught him sleeping with the babysitter. I'm not sure what I would do if it weren't for my mother. She's caring for them while I struggle here in this infernal diner."

I move my enormous hat that covers my face. She takes a closer look at me.

"Why, you're Claire Devine! We love your show. Mother and I are Evenings of Our Lives fans. I read in the newspaper that you're filming at the Christmas tree farm. My father used to work there."

My devilish nature emerges from my Tiger Lady persona.

"Here's a nice little tip to help you out." I give her my big fat expensive engagement ring.

"This is a beautiful ring. Why would you give me something few people can afford?"

"I don't like the way your husband treated you. You deserve it. You can probably get a pretty penny for this at your local pawn shop."

"Wow, my lucky day. You're the same person as you are on Evenings of Our Lives. I love you. See my fingernails? They have your nail polish on them."

"They look spectacular. Remember, Stage Fright Cosmetics Give You Confidence."

I get a big smile.

"Make sure the guy I came with, who is on a phone call now, pays the check when he comes back. Tell him I already covered the tip."

When Logan finds out that the engagement is off and I don't return his ring, he tries to sue me to get the ring back. All the negative press from this move gets him fired from the show. I told him I gave the ring to the waitress as a tip. She told him she hocked it at a local pawn shop. The pawn shop said that they sold it to someone. He was out of luck. One of the many fine directors lobbying for his job gets it. It gives me great satisfaction knowing that Logan will make payments on the ring for the next ten years, and that I will not be his golden ticket to becoming an executive producer. I hate being used. Hopefully, the Country Boy Diner waitress can now afford a few nice things for her family.

51. Emma's Graduation

"Pomp and Circumstance sound great from the orchestra playing it in the pit," I comment to Thomas and Megan.

I ask the woman sitting next to me, "Where did that orchestra come from?"

"Massachusetts Institute of Technology has an orchestra program; my son plays the bassoon. So, he's a dual major in music and mechanical engineering."

"Wow," I say, "I'm impressed."

"My sister's graduating today too. She just earned her Ph.D. in astrophysics."

"Congratulations are for all of us," says Megan.

As Emma walks on stage in her fancy doctoral robe, the announcer states, "Emma Hall, Ph.D. astrophysics and the Barrett Prize winner for her deep space exploration research."

She stands next to the president of MIT and shakes his hand.

"The MIT administration has doubled her $1,000 Barrett Prize to $2,000 because Ms. Hall has pledged to give all her prize money to the Emma's Wish Foundation to help eliminate homelessness."

There's a standing ovation.

The woman says, "You must be especially proud today."

"We certainly are, as I'm sure you are too," Megan responds.

Thomas stands there gleaming and shaking his head in wonderment.

After the ceremony, we go to Legit Sea Foods for dinner.

"Isn't this the famous place where Palmer vomited on Carla's Hot Red Dress?" I ask.

"This is it," says Megan. "I had to visit this place as I heard so much about it from Alex."

"I heard all about it too," says Emma. "Palmer Grandstone is the biggest horse's ass in the world. He's so full of himself that it's pathetic. I think he was spying on Zach and me in his rented Lincoln

Continental a decade ago. Palmer Grandstone wanted Alex, and Ray Fish to harm Ben because Ben is a women's rights advocate. I'll never understand why they were spying on me."

"They work together," I say. "Ray and Palmer are a team. Perhaps they had a nefarious plan to use you to get what they wanted."

Thomas changes the subject, "Emma, what are your plans now?"

"I have some excellent news. I've accepted an internship at NASA and will work with the James Webb Space Telescope team. They've been working on this extraordinary telescope for years."

"Tell us more," Thomas implores.

"It will see right into stellar nurseries, where stars and their planetary systems are being born. The observations will answer questions about how the clouds of dust and gas collapsed to form stars and how these planetary systems formed around them. It will see about ten to fifteen billion light-years away, and it will be about one hundred times more powerful than Hubble."

"Holy smokes," I say. "Will we find answers to the origins of the universe?"

"We don't yet know what we'll discover, but it will be astounding whatever we see."

"On an earthlier note, how's Zach?" Megan asks.

"I've meant to tell you this, but we broke up. We decided our paths are different, and we're not ready for marriage."

"That's sad," Thomas says.

"Theo," mom asks. "How's Claudia?"

"I've meant to tell you this, but we broke up. We decided our paths are different, and we're not ready for marriage."

"Twins think alike," says mom.

"I've learned one smart thing in my twenty-eight years," I say.

Everyone looks at me, expecting something brilliant.

"I've discovered that relationships are more complicated than the James Webb Space Telescope."

52. Floppy Flips Palmer

Damn, dogs are barking again. I buy this expensive home on Commonwealth Avenue, and a small, high-pitched screaming dog constantly barks. I can't stand it any longer! Ray Fish would know how to fix this problem.

I call him, "Ray, I need you to fix a major problem. If you do something for me, I'll pay your way to Boston."

"What do you want me to do?"

"You know about animals since you once owned a dairy farm. I have a problem with a dog in the Brownstone next to me. I called the city, and they don't think it's a nuisance. How do I stop this dog from barking?"

"The best way I know to stop a dog like this from barking is to kill it with no evidence."

"Ray, could you do this for me?"

"It'll cost you, Palmer. Nothing like this is free."

"I'll pay you ten thousand dollars plus expenses to come to Boston."

"I'm sorry, Palmer, that's not enough. You'll need to pay me twenty-five thousand dollars plus expenses to show you how to do it. I will not kill a little dog, but I'll show you how."

"That's too much money."

"Okay, Palmer, learn to enjoy the dog. Make the screeching sound of the annoying little pest your friend. You'll be better able to cope with it this way."

"I can't cope with it. The dog is killing me. Twenty-five it is. When can you come?"

"Let me check my schedule."

"Ray, are you still there?"

"Be patient Palmer, I'm looking at my calendar now. There, all done. I'm free for now. You'll have to buy me a first-class round-trip ticket, or I won't come."

"Why does it have to be a first-class ticket?"

"Do you ever fly first class, Palmer?"

"I only fly first class."

"As the Bible says, do unto others as you would do to yourself."

"You're incorrigible, Ray. Okay, I'll pay for your first-class ticket, but I won't pay you if your plan doesn't work."

"You must pay me upfront. But I guarantee results. After all, I used to own a dairy farm and know a lot about animals."

"Get over here as soon as possible. I want that little pest in dog heaven immediately, if not sooner!"

"Hey Palmer, we've been doin' business for a long time. I thought your family's been in Boston for generations. Weren't you raised here in the good old USA? Where'd you get that weird accent? You don't sound like no American."

"None of your stinking business, Ray. Now get on that damnable first-class flight and do your exorbitantly paid job!"

"Palmer, that was an amazing flight. They treated me like royalty. I enjoyed the free champagne, gourmet food, the imported Swiss chocolates, and the hot-lookin' stewardesses. I just thought you should know how grateful I am for treating me so well. Pay me in cash; then, I'll show you how to take care of the little doggie next door."

"Here is your stinking money, Ray. Now show me how to kill the dog."

"Let me count the money first. Looks good to me. Palmer, would you like some Swiss chocolate from my first-class flight? I pocketed some extras. They were non-stop and came with the first-class ticket price."

"No thanks, Ray; I don't want any chocolate now. I want to know how to stop that wild yapping annoyance next door."

"Palmer, I'm trying to show you how to take care of the problem next door. This is an expensive chocolate bar. Throw some of it over the fence for several nights, and the little doggie won't be a problem anymore. If you don't want to give the dog this expensive Swiss chocolate from my first-class flight, you can eat it yourself and get some cheap chocolate from your local convenience store."

"What? Chocolate will kill dogs?"

"Chocolate will take care of the little doggie."

"Why didn't you tell me this over the phone?"

"Nothing is free, pal, except for this stuff; it's quite expensive, and included in the cost of flying first class."

The brownstone next door gets a note on the front porch.

"Hi, I am an anonymous friend. Install a security camera on your fence line next to Palmer Grandstone's property as soon as possible—if not immediately. When Palmer throws things over the fence, don't let your dog eat any of them, but ensure that you get a good picture of him doing it. Collect what he throws over the fence. Make sure your cameras are good enough to see his face and the wrapper he's using and call the county dog patrol, or whatever you call it in Boston."

The sentencing:

"The evidence is incontrovertible. You attempted to kill the dog that was next to your property. I sentence you to six months of community service at the community dog park."

The dog park:

"What's your name?"

"Palmer Grandstone."

"Your job will be to pick up dog feces when the park closes until all the dog poop is gone. This is a community dog park, and we want it to be a splendid place for your neighbors to take their dogs."

Night shift:

I hate this place. I've been scooping up dog poop for three months now. At first, I wouldn't say I liked it. Now I hate it even more. I could kill Ray Fish. He promised the dog would die. Little did I know they had security cameras. It still barks all the time and echoes around my home. It has destroyed my privileged life. I'd rather hear little feet prancing around and a beautiful wife serving my needs than a high-pitched, never-ending barking dog!

Today is awful. I have achieved the pinnacle of success with my art store, only to have it destroyed by my instance upon making as much money as possible. Carla's right. Everything she said about me is true. I'm ashamed of myself. Artists are finding other stores to sell their artwork. My stupid decisions impugned my reputation. Here I am picking up dog feces. It's cold here too. I've never cried before. Why don't people pick up after their dogs? Lazy bastards.

Arf, Arf.

Go away little dog. Where did you come from?

Arf, Arf.

My God in heaven, you're so small.

Someone dropped off a stray dog in this park.

Just stop attempting to have me pick you up.

Arf, Arf.

It looks like you haven't eaten anything for weeks.

You're shaking; you're so cold.

No collar?

You can hardly bark, you're so weak, but your little tail is wagging.

You must be happy to see me; no one else is happy to see me.

Why, you may have more to cry about than I.

I have everything; you have nothing

I must take you home with me.

You can't stay out here all night long.

I'll take you to the shelter in the morning.

Welcome to my home, little dog.

What am I supposed to call you?

Your ears are rather floppy.

I think I'll call you Floppy for now.

I have some leftover chicken with peas and carrots I was going to eat tonight.

First, I'll get you some water.

My God, you're thirsty.

Here, have some of my dinner.

When was the last time you had something to eat?

Why, you wolfed half of my dinner down.

I guess you must poop too.

I'll let you run around in my courtyard for a spell.
Arf Arf.
I have dog poop bags in my pocket.
I'm an expert at picking up dog poop.
So, you want me to pick you up?
Okay. Stop snuggling your head under my chin.
It's not fair.
It's not appropriate for you and not suitable for me.
No one is snuggling their head under my chin except for you,
Floppy.
You need a bath.
You stink.
You'll fit well in my kitchen sink.
Why do you love this bath so much?
You want me to keep running warm water on you.
So, do you like my expensive French soap?
I'm tired.
I need to get ready for bed.
Stay here, Floppy, while I get ready for bed.
So, you don't want to be alone.
You follow me up the stairs to my bathroom.
I'm brushing my teeth now, Floppy.
You're just sitting there looking at me.
Can't I have any privacy?
Arf Arf.
I need to go to bed.
I arrange some towels on top of a pillow on the floor.
Now, lie here.
Stop whimpering.
You jumped on my bed.
My, you must have powerful legs.
What am I supposed to do now?
So, you curl up into a little ball by my feet.
Your hair is so short you must be cold.
There, this bath towel will make you all warm and cozy.
I can feel you with my feet.
Hum.
You warm my feet, Floppy.
My tears are gone.

I think I'm in love.

53. Annabel Annihilates Palmer

"No one has claimed Floppy, Mr. Grandstone. He's all yours. You must get him neutered, vaccinated, and licensed before we can release him to you."

"How do I take care of a dog?"

"Brush his teeth daily, give him a heartworm pill monthly, clip or get his toenails clipped regularly, walk him daily for exercise, and feed him a grain-free diet. Don't give him any kibble."

"What's kibble?" I ask.

"Dried hard dog food. But most of all, Mr. Grandstone, give him lots of love and attention."

I can't leave him home alone all day while at the galleries. So, I think I'll take him to work today and see what happens.

"Palmer," says my store greeter. "What a cute little dog. Where did you get him?"

"He was a stray at the dog park."

"He's so small and cuddly. Can I hold him?"

"Sure," I say.

"Palmer," she says, "I never thought of you as a dog owner. It's just not you. Did you rescue him?"

"I never thought I'd want a dog, but Floppy just happened. He was a stray. No one has claimed him."

"Please bring him here every day. The customers will love it."

Sure enough, walk-in traffic doubles in a month. Everyone is so taken with Floppy that they come back and buy something. Floppy greets them at the door, sniffs them, then backs off. Everywhere I go with Floppy, people go bonkers over him. At the outdoor seating area at Starbucks near my store, little Floppy attracts the most beautiful women I've ever seen. Why didn't I think of this before?

In walks a woman to my gallery with a short haircut like a man. She has a long dress on with sneakers. Not my type at all. She has a limp but gets around the store with no trouble. She stares at my favorite paintings for a long time.

"May I help you?" I ask.

"Not really, I can't afford any of these pictures, but I love them."

Floppy wanders up to us.

"Oh, what a beautiful dog," the woman exclaims.

"Can I pick him up?"

"Of course you can."

"Oh, what a cute little doggie," she exclaims with joy as Floppy snuggles his head under her chin.

"What's his name?"

"Floppy."

"What a cute name. Is this your dog?"

"Yes."

"Where did you get him?"

"He was a stray dog. So I just picked him up."

"You rescued little Floppy?"

"Yes."

"You're a wonderful man."

I think to myself, "No one has ever called me wonderful before. I've been called narcissistic, self-centered, greedy, and a pig, but never wonderful. A strange feeling surges through me."

"If you ever need a dog sitter, I would be thrilled to oblige."

"I'll keep you in mind. Do you have a business card?"

She pulls out a card. It says, "Dog Heaven. Boarding for the day or extended periods."

I examine the card. "Dog Heaven is on the South Side?"

"Yes. My mother and I live there. I moved from California recently to care for her—she's ill. I take care of her and earn extra money by dog sitting. The dogs are therapeutic for mom. I only take small dogs under twenty pounds. Several of our dogs are recovering from accidents, are old, and no one wants them, or we take dogs who need a foster home before going to a new family. We also take dogs like Floppy who need a place to stay when their owners can't be with them."

"I may need some help. May I visit Dog Heaven to see where Floppy might stay when I'm not home and can't take him with me?"

"Of course."

"May I come tomorrow?"

"Okay, how about tomorrow evening if your day job is here?"

"What's your name?" I ask.

"Annabelle."

I was about to tell her my name, but her phone rang.

"I must go. See you at eight tomorrow night."

Six little dogs are on her huge couch when I walk into their humble old home. As she said, they all look like they've been in car accidents or are old. Some have bandages on them; others look up at Floppy and me without doing much—except for wagging their tails. Annabelle's mother is sitting in an old rocking chair. A tube reaches her nose attached to an oxygen concentrator machine.

"Mom, this is… I'm sorry, I don't know your name."

"Palmer," I say.

If I tell them my last name, they may not take Floppy with all of Carla's publicity and the Red-Hot Dress scandal.

"Palmer, this is my mom, Judy."

"Nice to meet you, Palmer."

"The same," I respond.

"What a cute little doggie. May I hold the bundle of love?"

"Of course." Floppy takes to Judy like a fly to flypaper. He snuggles himself into every crevice of her frail body.

"Let me show you around."

Annabelle takes me to their tiny little fenced backyard, where the dog's poop and exercise. Eagle eye I am now for dog poop; I don't see any.

"Looks like you keep this space clean."

"Yep."

"What did you do in California?"

"I worked as a guard in the municipal museum in LA. I love art and could observe the masters all day long."

I couldn't keep myself from finding Annabelle and her mother endearing. I've never in my life given thought to compassion or caring—except for myself. This Annabelle woman is the sweetest thing, caring for her mother and helpless dogs. How could anything be more beautiful? She's a plain-looking woman. No makeup. Short hair. She must have had an accident, as she has a limp. I dare not ask her about her limp—maybe later.

"I'm sold. I plan to be out of town next week. Can you take Floppy then?"

"Drop her off on Monday morning, please. Don't you want to know how much I charge?"

"How much do you charge?"

"Fifty dollars per day."

"Fine. I'll see you on Monday."

As I drive home, feelings surge through me I never knew existed. A plain-looking woman with short hair and a limp is more beautiful than all the art I have ever observed. What's wrong with me?

"Annabelle, do you know who that is?"

"Palmer, a nice guy who works in an art store."

"Annabelle, he owns the art gallery you visited. That's Palmer Grandstone. He's famous in Boston. I've been following him in the newspaper for years."

"He can afford fifty dollars per day then. I have to go out for a spell and will get home in time to get you to bed."

"You're an angel, Annabelle. Have fun. I'll tell you about Palmer Grandstone gossip later."

"Frankly, mom, I don't want to know. He seems like a nice guy. Anyone who has so much love for a dog that he rescued is okay with me."

"Okay, dear, it's probably best that you don't know."

"Yep. I hate gossip."

54. She's Engaged

Claire's engaged. I must forget her. It was stupid of me to go to Vermont looking for her. She was always getting in my way to get my attention. She had curly red hair and this eternal smile on her face. We became good friends. Both of us got into the Portland Youth Philharmonic and even practiced scales together. We ate lunch in the school cafeteria together; went on walks together; we even went to the prom together. Her curly red hair turned into long sexy red hair that millions of adoring fans must love on television. She's famous now and engaged to a movie director. Our relationship is toast.

I look at the picture she gave me in the Vermont coffee shop. I took this picture of her when we walked to a beautiful park near Dunthorpe—Elk Rock Garden. The park overlooks the Willamette River. It was the one thing that reminded me of home when I was in my tent. She's just standing on the bridge with colorful wildflowers in the background. She was always there for me. How could I have been so cruel to reject her? Ben tried to warn me when he told me how he made such stupid decisions at my age. My ambition blinded me. I was so selfish and self-centered that I rejected the most beautiful woman in the world. What a fool I've been. She wrote her phone number on the back of the picture and asked me to call her. How in the hell did she ever get this picture? Did she have time to snoop around my tent when she found me out cold on the sidewalk?

There's nothing like playing in the New York Philharmonic, but I feel like I did after playing Tchaikovsky's Violin Concerto in D with the Portland Youth Phil. I'm still alone on a comfortable train looking out the window to see a devastated landscape. I remember having dinner at the Heathman Hotel with tablecloths and cloth napkins. Tea served in China pots, and bow-tied servers serving gourmet food. The only thing separating our privilege from the homeless people in the street is a giant picture window. Emma couldn't stand it, and we had to leave. She wanted to know how we could look at hungry, cold, people while eating in luxury. This scene inspired my billionaire stepfather, Thomas, to start up Emma's Wish.

I'm now in the lap of luxury, compared to the people I met when I lived in Tent City, even though I can barely afford this apartment in New York City. Fortunately, I'm seeing some royalties from Blast. What a dichotomy. Do I have any purpose and meaning in life? I must get off this luxury train to nowhere. Where do I begin? I look at the picture again. Claire, Claire, I love you. I always have, but I was too stupid to see what was right before my eyes. Ben was right. The wall phone was staring at him in the grocery store during an active robbery, but he was too stupid to make the call. Claire has been right there before me since I was ten, but I was too stupid to make the call.

What if I was engaged, and some flame from the past stalked me and wanted to rekindle things? Claire's engaged. I must forget her.

55. Mass Shooter

I don't like to take the subway home after concerts but prefer to take the bus. I feel safer on a bus than in the subway tunnels at night. The only seat I can find on this bus is an aisle seat. So, I sit next to an older woman. I have my violin strapped to my back in its thirty-pound solid steel case. I take it off to sit; it's now on my lap.

"Do you play the violin?" the lady asks.

"Yes," I answer.

"Where?"

"In the New York Philharmonic."

"That must be a wonderful experience," she says. "I used to play the violin but gave it up years ago. My daughter is a pianist. She plays jazz in supper clubs and used to play at the Top of the Sixes, but it closed. She's a solo act and entertains New Yorkers as they dine and drink."

"Where does she play now?" I ask.

But before she can answer, we hear gunshots in the back of the bus. A shooter just shot a passenger, then another one. He keeps shooting as he walks back toward the front of the bus! He has a nylon stocking pulled over his head.

He's yelling, "Die liberal, Jew, big city Democrat mother fuckers. Die, die, die!"

His machine gun fills the bus with gun smoke. Bullets fly. Windows shatter.

People are screaming and ducking their heads down. I remember Fred's foot, so I take a gamble. Like Ben told me, I don't want to be a stupid teenager, so I stick my foot out into the aisle, just like Fred did to me in the freezing rain. When the guy walks by backward, he trips on my foot, falls, and loses control of his gun. He starts to get up, grabs his gun from the floor of the bus, and points it at me. I take my solid steel violin case, using its back straps as a handle, lift it, and as it goes down, he pulls the trigger. The bullet ricochets off the violin case as my case smashes down on his head. He's lifeless. People are struggling, wounded, screaming, and panicked—or dead.

The lady I sat next to points at me and shouts to everyone, "I saw the whole thing; he's a hero. He tripped the shooter and hit him on the head with his violin case."

Then, the mayhem subsides as people on the bus clap.

Flashing police and emergency vehicle lights are everywhere. Finally, the police arrive with guns dressed in riot gear and Kevlar vests. Police cars surround the bus and cordon off the street. Eventually, paramedics come into the bus, assess the damage, and carry the dead and wounded out in stretchers. The woman that I sat next to tells the police everything that happened.

New York Times Headline:
Passenger Kills Deadly Mass Shooter on New York City Bus
The article reads:

"Theo Hall, a New York Philharmonic Violin player, and composer killed a mass shooter by tripping him and then using his violin case to hit him on the head. The shooter tried to kill Mr. Hall, but his bullet ricocheted off his solid steel violin case. Risking his own life, he saved countless lives with quick wit and bravery. The shooter, Edward Griffin, from Pampa, Texas, executed several mass shootings. He killed 76 people in surprise attacks like this in New York City, Philadelphia, and Boston. Griffen vowed to attack big-city liberals, Democrats, and Jews. Mr. Hall foiled the gunman's attempt to kill him and others by shielding himself with his solid steel violin case and then killing the gunman with it by hitting him on the head."

The major news television networks all want to interview me. When I go to the Lincoln Center for a New York Philharmonic rehearsal a few days later, television cameras and reporters won't leave me alone. They all want to interview me separately, shoving cameras and mikes into my face. I struggle to get to the back door entrance and turn around to answer questions.

The first reporter from NBC asks, "What were you thinking when you tripped the shooter?"

"I was thinking about when someone tripped me and how helpless I was. I almost lost my ability to play the violin because of my hand injury. It still bothers me to this day."

A gorgeous young reporter from CNN with long brunette hair asks me, "What was the deciding factor in attempting to subdue the shooter?"

"My pastor in Portland, Oregon, once told me how stupid he was for not acting when two armed robbers robbed the grocery store, he was working in; they were also wearing nylon stockings pulled over their heads. He could have called 911 in the back of the store, as the wall phone was right in front of him. Instead, he went up to the front of the store, near the cash registers to see what was happening only to have a gun pointed at him. All this went through my mind when I saw the shooter with a nylon stocking pulled over his head as a disguise. My pastor regretted not doing anything and told me how stupid he had been. I didn't want to follow in his footsteps."

The reporter gives me her card, Natasha Galkin, CNN News. I put it in my pocket.

I face the reporters at the top of the stairs, "Thank you all for reporting on this. I must get into a rehearsal. I'm late."

The Lincoln Center security guard escorts me in. When I walk into the rehearsal, it stops. Everyone stands and claps longer than the standing ovation I received when I played Tchaikovsky's Violin Concerto in D with the Portland Youth Philharmonic a decade ago.

When I get home, I pull the card out of my pocket, and on the back, Natasha Galkin from CNN writes, "Call me. A good man is hard to find."

It's all over the news. I feel like a rock star while fighting the women off. I enjoy all the attention at first, but deep down, the only woman I love beyond all measure is Claire with the beautiful red hair.

56. Palmer Recognizes Theo

Having coffee at my favorite coffee shop, next to my art gallery, is my favorite time of day. Floppy always attracts people; I love it when he attracts beautiful women. I can't believe I'm not interested in them. But unfortunately, I can't get Annabelle out of my mind. With short manly hair, a limp, and no makeup, what's inside of her makes my heart thump. Her rescue dogs in her mother's humble home haunt me. This extraordinary woman loves rescue dogs and helps her elderly mother, who relies on an oxygen machine to breathe.

I see a Boston newspaper that someone abandoned on their now-empty table. I can't help but notice the headline, "Theo Hall, Violinist, and Composer Kills Deadly Mass Shooter on New York City Bus."

I wonder if it's the same mass shooter that was in Boston? Theo Hall was Alexandria's star student! She turned Theo Hall into an international star, and he became a national hero. Another article reports that the New York Philharmonic orchestra will be performing in Boston for the first time since 1999.

I speed-dial Dog Heaven.

"Annabelle, would you like to go to a concert with me? The New York Philharmonic is performing in Boston for the first time since 1999. Theo Hall, the hero in New York who killed the mass shooter, plays violin in the orchestra. I know him indirectly."

"How do you know Theo Hall indirectly?"

"Well, in a nutshell, I played clarinet in the Boston Youth Symphony as a teenager. Then, as an adult, I became engaged to a girl who played in the Boston Youth Symphony with me. The engagement ended in utter failure. She was Theo Hall's violin teacher for many years."

"Okay. Sounds like fun." Annabelle answers.

57. Stalking Theo in Boston

Our sneaky plan takes shape. I wait at the back door of Symphony Hall. Carla's waiting by the front entrance, where she may 'accidentally' bump into Theo. There's only one rear door, so I hang out here after the performance.

Carla and I are on our phones together. It's cold standing out here.

Carla says, "I haven't seen him yet."

Musicians exit from the back door. I must keep an eagle eye out for him. Finally, he walks out with his violin case on his back. I follow him to the coffee shop and inform Carla where it is. He's sitting in a booth by himself with a baseball cap on to disguise his face from everyone.

When we walk in, he sees us, and we look surprised.

Carla and I say in unison, "Theo, what a surprise!"

Theo says, "Yah, what a surprise!"

Just as we're about to pretend to act normal, Carla's eyes widen.

"Keep your heads down," Carla says.

We get into the booth with Theo.

"That's Palmer Grandstone in the expensive suit," she whispers. "Keep your heads down so he won't notice us."

We're too late. Palmer notices us with the other flipped-out customers in the coffee shop by seeing all of us in one place.

- Claire Devine, Evenings of Our Lives actress
- Carla Furbee, the Boston Symphonic Red-Hot Dress oboe player
- Palmer Grandstone, a famous Boston art store owner, who vomited on Carla Furbee's Red-Hot Dress at Legit Sea Foods
- A mystery woman with Palmer Grandstone
- Theo Hall, the New York Philharmonic musician, composer, and national hero who killed a deadly mass shooter

Everyone in the coffee shop is clamoring for autographs from all of us and taking pictures. Palmer and Annabelle squeeze into the booth with us. Finally, the manager of the coffee shop asks everyone to back off so the celebrities can enjoy a cup of coffee.

"Palmer, who's the lady with you?" Carla asks.

"This is Annabelle. She's my dog sitter."

Carla gasps, "You have a dog? Is that your dog in that pouch?"

"Yes," Palmer answers.

"What a cute little puppy. What's the dog's name?" I ask.

"Floppy," Annabelle answers.

"Did you attend the concert?" Theo asks, "If so, how did you get Floppy in the concert hall?"

"See this pouch. Floppy fits in here, and no one even asked. He's a little angel wherever I go," Palmer brags.

Carla utters in disbelief, "This is strange, Palmer. You own a dog. I don't get it. I thought you hated all small and cuddly things?"

Palmer responds, "It's a long, long story I'm not proud of. Do you want to hear it?"

"Yes, Yes," we all respond in unison.

"They forced me to work for the animal protective services for attempting to kill, with chocolate, the annoying, barking dog living next door to my home. They assigned me to a dog park for six months to pick up dog feces for my sentence."

Everyone sits here in silent disbelief at Palmer's heart-felt disclosure.

Theo breaks the silence. "I applaud you. Palmer, for making the best of an unpleasant situation. I learned a few things living in Tent City, like respect for people less fortunate than me, and how uncomfortable situations, entirely of our own making, can change our lives."

Palmer says, "Humility and a love for dogs were some of the things I learned. I found a dog with no home and no one to love him, much like my pathetic love life, at the dog park. Someone just left him there alone. He was helpless and needed a home. I adopted him. I bring him to Grandstone Galleries daily, and the customers love him too."

I ask, "Where did the name, Floppy, come from?"

"Just look at his cute little ears," Palmer replies. "They flop around when he walks or runs. My little Floppy puts his head under my chin when his ears are cold to warm them up."

Annabelle says, "Floppy does that with my mom because he loves her, not just to keep his ears warm."

We all laugh at her humor.

Mostly silent up to this point, Carla fumes, "This isn't the Palmer Grandstone I grew up with and had to deal with as an adult. I'm having a hard time believing all this sanctimonious drivel— exacerbated by your strange high-brow accent that gets worse as you get older. You made Alex's life and my life miserable for many years. I'd like to go to the ladies' room and vomit but can't because of the cameras."

Carla sits there in silence again.

Palmer says, "Carla, I'm so sorry for being such an arrogant, narcissistic fool through the years. Will you forgive me?"

Carla says nothing. Silence ensues.

To break the uncomfortable silence I ask, "Annabelle, how did you meet Palmer?"

Annabelle says, "I was looking at the art in Palmer's store and met him, not knowing he owns the place, and Floppy, who greets the customers in his store, introduced himself to me. I'm a dog sitter, and the rest is history."

"Theo," Palmer says, "You're so quiet when you stopped a mass shooter in his tracks, overcame a debilitating hand injury, and wrote a major symphonic work. The main reason we're here tonight is that I read all about you in the newspaper. We came to see you perform."

My humble hero Theo says nothing.

A cute girl throws a white embroidered handkerchief at Theo in the booth behind us. He picks it up off the table, turns to look at her, smiles, and says, "Thank you, me lady." She blushes.

They point the cameras at us, and customers send pictures all over social media.

Annabelle chimes in, "I'm outta here. I'm not used to all this fame, publicity, and just plain weirdness. See ya all later, bye."

As she attempts to leave the coffeehouse, a reporter walks in with a camera operator and sticks a microphone in her face.

The reporter asks, "You came here with Palmer Grandstone and are now leaving without him. Who are you?"

Annabelle struggles to escape the coffee shop while the paparazzi mobs it. They caught wind that Claire Devine, Theo Hall, Carla Furbee, Palmer Grandstone, and a mystery woman were all in the same place at once.

"What's your relationship with Palmer Grandstone? What's your name? Where do you live?"

"Please leave me alone," Annabelle begs all of them, pushing them away.

Theo, my hero, gets out of the booth and asks them to leave her alone.

The Paparazzi have so much respect for Theo that they back off of Annabelle but point their cameras at Theo; he avoids them and shields Annabelle from the hordes of Paparazzi and legitimate news reporters with his violin case. We all follow him out with cameras pointed at us too. Theo hails a taxi, and we all squeeze in. It's so crowded that I get to sit on Theo's lap in the back. I can tell he's extra happy to have me here.

58. True Confessions

After the coffee shop debacle, the cab takes Annabelle and Palmer to the parking garage where Palmer's Mercedes is located; it takes Claire and Carla to Carla's home. The taxi takes me to the hotel the symphony provided for our Boston concert.

About midnight, my phone rings. It's Claire. She asks me, "Did you know that the last time we went on a date was to the senior prom?"

"Are you asking me out for a date?"

"Of course, silly goose. Don't you want to see me again?"

It didn't take me long to answer, "Where, when?"

"Tomorrow?" Claire suggests.

"I don't have to take the symphony bus back; I could always stay in Boston for a few days. Why don't you come to my hotel room, and we can order from room service. This way, we don't have to deal with unwanted publicity."

"Stellar idea," Claire agrees.

The next day, I hear a knock on the door. Claire's so beautiful I can hardly stand it. She's just standing there outside my hotel room wearing the same simple spaghetti strap black dress, with black pumps, a pearl necklace, and pearl earrings she wore to the prom a decade ago.

"Claire, where'd you get that dress?"

"I knew we'd be getting together, so I bought it with me. It's been my go-to little black dress for years. So, I thought you might like it."

"My God. You look spectacular in that dress. Just as you did at the prom."

"Gee whiz, thanks, Theo."

"I have a surprise," I say.

"What?"

"There's a private room in the hotel restaurant downstairs that I have reserved, and I have another surprise."

"Really?" Claire questions

"I still wear the same jacket that I wore to the prom, and I just happen to have it in my suitcase if I need to go out to a nice place for dinner." I put it on, and Claire laughs, giggles, and cries all at the same time.

"Great minds think alike," she says.

In the private dining room, we order our food. We both order the Pacific Northwest wild-caught King salmon.

Claire declares, "I can't believe we're in Boston and order something that's shipped here when we can get this in Portland, near the coast, where it's caught. I miss Portland."

"Me too," I agree.

"Claire, I have a confession to make. We didn't run into each other in Vermont accidentally. I saw you on Evenings of Our Lives. I knew you were an actress and wanted to run into you."

"That's sneaky and terrible, Theo, but I have a few other confessions."

She starts counting on her index finger.

"One, I saw you hiding behind a newspaper in the coffee shop. I couldn't stop thinking about you since then. Two, I saw you in the forest hiding behind the trees; I almost forgot my lines. Three, I had to pretend I didn't know all this the following day again in the coffee shop. Four, I acted surprised when you told me you were in the New York Philharmonic; I already knew this."

"How did you know?" I ask.

"I still talk to your mom now and then, and she filled me in. Five, we didn't run into each other by chance in Boston. Carla and I hatched a plan to run into you 'accidentally on purpose' after the concert. She waited at the front entrance, and I waited at the back."

"Claire, that's sneaky and terrible, but I have another confession. I was in the lobby of Symphony Hall and saw Carla hanging out in the front, talking on her phone. Something was up, so I went to the back entrance and saw you hiding out across the street also on your phone. I walked to the coffee shop, ensuring that you could see me. When you both walked in, I had to act as you did in Vermont. Did I do an excellent job of acting?"

"You did a terrible job of acting, Theo. When we were in grade school, you'd always tap your foot when lying. You were tapping your foot the entire time in the Vermont cupcake shop, and as soon as we walked into the coffee shop after the concert in Boston, your foot was tapping the entire time."

"So, we both stalked each other, and I'm a terrible actor," I lament.

"Theo, why didn't you call me after I gave you my phone number?"

"I didn't want to get in the way. Your big fat ring sparkled like a blinding light that said, 'I'm taken, back off.'"

"Theo, it's like you to be such a considerate gentleman. You were like this in grade school. Even if I bumped into you to get your attention, you'd apologize. How could any girl not fall in love with a sweet guy like you? But you just didn't feel the same way about me, so I bailed on the relationship. You were busy with Claudia, and I had to live my life without you."

"I am so stupid; I can hardly stand it. Ben tried to tell me, but I was too stupid to understand how stupid I was. Ten years have passed. Both of us have learned much about life. Here we are together again."

"Yep."

"Claire, I have another question. How'd you get the picture of you I hung in my tent behind the flap?"

Claire looks pensive and says, "You must know nothing about the incident."

"What incident?" I ask.

"It's a long story," Claire says.

She tells me about Brett, Donald, and Gym and how it scared the hell out of her, how she took self-defense lessons from Belle Brown, how she looked for evidence with Ben in Tent City, how they found my old tent, how Dick Wolf attempted to rape her, and how she scratched his eye out with her tiger claw.

"You blinded him in one eye with your tiger claw?"

"Remember, I take self-defense lessons from Belle Brown— Ben's self-defense instructor. Whenever she visits Carla in Boston or whenever I visit Portland, she always gives me more and more lessons. I'm a fierce animal Theo. I'm a Tiger Lady; no one messes with me. But, of course, as a famous actress, I could hire a full-time bodyguard or know how to defend myself."

Claire opens her purse and pulls out her tiger claw. "I never leave home without this. I told you about my tiger claw when you were in the hospital, but you were so out of it you probably don't remember."

I'm stunned, "Dick Wolf, the same asshole who hit me on the head?"

"Yep. The Dick Wolf with the brown teeth, skull and crossbones, tattoo on his neck, and a sickening face."

"I knew he was in prison for assaulting me, but I didn't know that you were the anonymous woman he attempted to rape in my old tent!"

"Well, now you know."

"Claire, I'm so sorry I caused everyone who loves me such trouble and pain. You're so cool. You risked your life for me?"

I've never cried before. It's such a strange feeling. Tears are streaming down my face as I realize she was always there and is here now, right in front of my eyes.

"Theo, you destroyed your violin hand for me and saved my life. What else was I supposed to do?"

I feel like a big stupid baby. Claire has loved me forever and risked her life for me; and all I could think about was myself.

"Theo, one question that I have for you has troubled me for years."

"What?" I ask.

"Why did you have that picture of me in your tent?"

"I guess it made me feel normal. You were always there, and without you being there, I felt like there was a void in my life. You were the one thing that kept me from feeling like I was on a 'train to nowhere' with a devastated landscape passing by. When I looked at the picture of you it made me feel like I was on a 'train to somewhere' and the landscape was beautiful—like you."

"Why didn't you tell me this, or respond to my persistent overtures of love and affection?"

"Because I didn't put two and two together. Ben tried to tell me, but I was too stupid to understand the deeper meaning of his words."

"That's flattering, Theo. I don't know what to say, except that you really are stupid."

We laugh.

"I have a question for you, Claire."

"Shoot."

"Where did the giant, blazing, stay-away-from-me ring go?

"I gave it to a single waitress as a tip, who pawned it, so she could take care of her two kids. Then I dumped him. The pawnshop sold it and Logan has to pay for it for the next ten years. When I saw you in the cupcake shop, so many feelings flooded me. I haven't stopped thinking about you since then."

"The same thing happened to me, but that damn ring kept getting in the way. Logan's an ass. I guess I have another question."

"Shoot," Claire says.

"How on earth did you say yes to a marriage proposal from Logan?"

"Theo, I guess I'm as stupid as you are."

"No one is stupid as me, and Ben of course. You probably had a list of pros and cons and made the best decision you could at the time counting on your fingers. But I just make stupid decisions without putting much thought into them."

"I agree," Claire declares.

"Where to from here?" I ask.

She looks at me with wet eyes and says, "Kiss me Theo."

I gleefully comply.

59. No One Messes with Claire

The entire cast of Evenings of Our Lives must appear at a big
gala at a Boston hotel. My production company wants me to go to
this gathering to schmooze with everyone for "positive public
relations." We're shooting in Vermont, so Boston is the largest city
for something like this to happen. They want me to pose in front of a
staged background for the press. Other cast members must do the
same. I'm exhausted from the commotion and from wearing high
heels all night. I go to my room and flop down on the bed without
even taking my shoes off. There's a knock on the door. I get up and
look through the peephole, and Herbert Weiner, the biggest
executive movie producer in the country, is staring at me. He was at
the gala and said he would get with me for some good news. How he
found out where my room is, I'll never know. When you're as rich as
he is, you can have anything. I open the door.

"Claire," he says, "Can we have a word?"

"Sure, I'll meet you down in the lobby," I attempt to close
the door.

He pushes the door open forcefully and walks in.

"Nice room," he says. "I have a proposition for you."

"Can we do this in the lobby?"

"Nah, he says. This won't take long."

"Do you know who I am?"

"Of course, Herbert Weiner; you own Weiner Films."

"Do you know who owns Evenings of Our Lives?"

"Weiner Films," I reply.

"Do you want to become a genuine movie star rather than a
slippery soaper?"

"I'm not sure what you're getting at, Mr. Weiner."

"You're a spectacularly beautiful woman, Claire. I have a role
that will launch you as a major movie star in real theaters, rather than
a silly soap opera."

"What is it?" I ask.

"Peter Feldman wrote the screenplay. He wrote screenplays for six major films starring all of our favorite actors and actresses."

"I saw all of them," I say.

"You could have the starring role that should make you more popular than Vivien Leigh. We have a budget of one hundred and fifty million dollars for this film of which you could be the lead."

"Show me the contract," I say.

"You must do a few things before we sign any papers."

He pulls down his pants and masturbates in front of me. With one hand on his penis, he attempts to push me down on the bed. My tiger claw is in my purse, but Belle has embedded her kicking exercises in my brain. I practice them now and then to keep in shape if something happens again. I even attended several Radio City Rockette shows to see how high and powerful they can kick. This asshole doesn't know what's about to happen to him.

"What's wrong, sweetheart? Don't you want the lead role in this movie? If you take care of papa, he'll take care of you. Do what I say, or it's all over with your soap and any future work in the movie business, of which I'm king."

I stand and get my bearings back after being pushed. I still had my high heels on. He comes at me once again. With all my training from Belle, when she pushed dummies at me countless times, I kick him in the face as hard as I can. Unfortunately, the pointy toe of my shoe misses his face, but the spiked heel goes right through his nose and rips his nostril out.

He screams, "My nose, my nose!"

I go into the hallway and call 911, watching Weiner hold his nose while staring at me in disbelief.

"Your career is over, bitch. My lawyers are powerful."

"Seriously? Here I am calling 911 for you, and you're planning on destroying my career because I stopped you from raping me? You're a genuine piece of work, Weiner. Fuck you."

Before the police arrive, he pulls his pants back on. He can't do anything to me, as he's now lying on the bed, whining with pain and holding his nose. I wait outside the room. The police and paramedics come at the same time.

Weiner points to me, telling them I kicked him with my shoe unprovoked. They read me my rights and take me away in handcuffs for allegedly assaulting Weiner. The paramedics take Weiner to the hospital.

I make my one phone call in jail to Jeremy Smith's cell phone. He gave me his phone number in case something like this should happen while I'm in Boston. He's now the chief investigator of the Boston police department. Twenty minutes later, he shows up, and after a few words with the staff, they let me go into his custody. We go directly to the crime scene, where the police are waiting for him. They cordoned the hotel room off with police tape.

"Tell me what happened?" Jeremy asks.

"Weiner knocked on the door, said who he was, and I opened it. He forced his way in, telling me how he could make me more famous than Vivien Leigh. Then he masturbates while pushing me on the bed."

"Did he ejaculate?"

"I'm not sure," I answer.

We see blood on the bed from his nose. Jeremy couldn't find any semen but found several pubic hairs. Jeremy picks them up with a pair of tweezers. A few days later we find out that his pubic hairs match his DNA perfectly.

After everything that happened, I find out that I'm one of Weiner's eighty-seven accusers. Many of them are much more famous than me—some are just getting started. Weiner messed with the wrong woman. I contacted every single accuser. We all pooled our money and hired the most prestigious law firm in the country. Weiner is now in jail for the rest of his life with only one nostril. Each of us received from one hundred thousand to a million dollars in compensation, depending on the severity of his actions. I gave all my compensation to the National Organization for Women.

60. Let's move back to Portland

I ask Claire, "What would you think if we just moved back to Portland and see what happens?"

"Theo, we've had some difficulties since moving to the East Coast. We're both famous and can't go anywhere without crowds."

"I'm not even sure that I want a life of fame. My violin case is even famous now."

Claire giggles. I love the way she laughs. "We need to laugh more. I feel sorry for people like Joshua Bell and Hilary Hahn. They're on the road constantly. How can they have a family?"

"Theo, did I hear you say, family?"

"Did I say that?"

"Since grade school, Theo, I've loved you more than anything. But that you mention the word 'family' is truly shocking."

I respond, "I guess we're at a crossroads. We don't have to enter the family thing for a few more years. Would you consider going back to Portland?"

"Did I just hear you say 'family' again?"

"Did I?"

"Yes. You did."

"It must be something that has changed inside of me. Even though my father wasn't too involved in my life, my stepfather is more like a real father; I wouldn't want to discount the whole idea of having a family of my own—someday."

"Theo, I'm shocked. You've made a big turnaround."

I ponder Claire's observation. "Life just happened. Blast just happened. You just happened. I guess my 'turnaround' just happened."

"It wouldn't be a bad idea to move back to Portland. My mom doesn't denigrate me anymore; I think she's making a turnaround. I have many BFFs in Portland who knew me before becoming famous. The headquarters of Stage Fright Cosmetics is in Portland, and Emily could use the help."

"Don't you help her enough by being the face of the company? Without your fame and television presence, Stage Fright Cosmetics wouldn't be what it is today."

"I'm just unsure if I want to remain in the spotlight all the time, and tired of watching my back wherever I go. I want some anonymity just like you did when you ended up in Tent City."

"Claire, you and I are only thirty years old. You already have an acting career that anyone would envy. You could probably get Evenings of our Lives to move to Portland. Stage Fright Cosmetics is hugely successful because of your star status. I could write music anywhere, even in a tent. After all, my entry into composing started in a tent. I have to choose. I can't write music and be full time in the New York Philharmonic. Because of my hand injury, I will never play the way I want. But with composing music, the sky's the limit."

"I have an idea," Claire proposes. "We could move to Portland and do good things for the community, and on the national stage, we could use whatever gifts and advantages we have."

"Exactly." I say, "Let's make a list of good things we can do and still pursue our talents."

"Theo, I need a pen to write down some thoughts about our plans."

"Look in my desk drawer," I say.

Claire looks in my desk drawer and pulls out the business card from the reporter who wrote on the back, "Call me. A good man is hard to find."

Claire presents the card to me and says, "I know Natasha Galkin from CNN. Before she shifted to news, she covered popular TV shows on another network. I had coffee with her while she interviewed me for a segment on my acting career. She's hot, Theo, and won't go out with just anyone. She looks like a model for Glamor Magazine and uses my nail polish. Did you take her up on a date?"

"I did."

"What was your date like?"

"She's nice, smart, beautiful, and thinks I'm the greatest thing ever to walk the face of the earth."

"So, what's the problem? Why are you not with her now?"

"She likes football and knows nothing about classical music. We have little in common. I looked through her record collection, filled with Taylor Swift, Justin Bieber, and Elvis Presley albums. If I had to listen to that stuff with her and watch football games, I might want to kill myself. She would always ask me what I was thinking and say, 'A penny for your thoughts' while presenting her bare ring finger. She would say, 'I'm from Missouri, where we get married.'"

"Hum," says Claire, "Sounds ominous."

"Claire, you're the only woman who understands me. No other woman but you mean so much to me. I could force myself to find love with another woman, but you take the cake. You love me and have loved me ever since I can remember. I can't think of any woman I would rather be with than you for the rest of my life."

"I've always felt that way about you, Theo, but you were too stupid to notice. Now that I have a pen, back to the list."

"I have a thought," I say. "I was looking up famous people who made a lasting contribution and still pursued their dreams. You wouldn't believe who popped up as an example.

"Who?" Claire questions.

"Danny Thomas."

"Why Danny Thomas?"

"Have you ever heard of St. Jude's Hospitals?" I ask.

"Of course. It all clicks in; Marlo Thomas is Danny Thomas's daughter. He started St. Jude's Hospitals, which is free, for all children who need care. Marlo is currently giving to the foundation."

"What about Paul Newman?" I ask. "One hundred percent of the profits from his food and beverage company go to charity. He felt he had been lucky in life, and sharing one's good fortune with others was, 'Just the right thing to do.' Perhaps I could carry on with Emma's wish, using my fleeting national fame to bolster it? Claire, you're currently contributing to Emma's wish through Stage Fright Cosmetics. Is there anything else you'd want to partner with?"

"The National Organization for Women would be a good start. With my experience fending off potential assaults, thanks to Belle Brown, women need all the support they can get."

"Good one," I agree. "Let's move back to Portland, enjoy Oregon's natural beauty, be near family and friends, pursue our dreams, and do something good for the world."

"I'm with you one hundred percent." Claire declares.

61. Give Back Initiative

"Thank you all for coming tonight to hear about Claire Devine and Theo Hall's Give Back Initiative. My name is Reverend Doctor Ben Dawson. Welcome to this beautiful facility that's now our permanent home. The Temple Beth Shalom congregation was a guest at the Lake Oswego Progressive Church of America for ten years while they searched for their own facility; tragically, our facility burned down. Shortly before it burned down, the Temple Beth Shalom congregation found this beautiful facility we are in now to gather. They invited us to stay here while we renovated our church. But Emma Hall came up with a brilliant idea that has come to fruition. Instead of rebuilding a new church, both congregations voted to keep sharing this building and partner to build a refugee resettlement center on our old property. Thank you, Emma."

Everyone claps.

"The Lake Oswego Progressive Church of America gathers on Sundays, and Temple Beth Shalom gathers on Saturdays. We think this is a much better use of our resources. This building is now occupied seven days a week, jointly shared by both congregations. Refugees seeking asylum from oppression have a place in Portland to safely integrate into the United States."

More clapping.

"Since people are here from all over Portland, there is room in the lower level with a live TV screen; you don't need to stand. Giving back will give you purpose and meaning in life no matter what path you pursue. We have invited the following people tonight as honored guests as they have affected Theo and Claire's life to become what they are today. Please stand and remain standing as I say your name:"

Ashley Rich-Fowler and Jay Fowler-Rich
Belle Brown
Alexandria Savich, and April Dawson
Brevard Hallstrom

Carla Furbee and Jeremy Smith
Claire Devine and Theo Hall
Claudia Hallstrom-Miller and David Miller-Hallstrom
Emily Young and Natalie Schrunk
Fred Freemark
Harold Sweeny
Janet and Bill Devine (Claire Devine's mother and father)
Megan Hall, Emma Hall, Thomas Harrison, and Lizzy
Nadia Jama and her parents
Palmer Grandstone, Annabelle, and Floppy

"Several of you have volunteered to share how you are or will give back. Please hold your applause until the end of the remarks."

"I introduce the following people:"

- Ashley Rich

"Theo Hall gave me confidence to do something with my life. I went to Portland State University as a Pre-Occupational Therapy major and ended up at Pacific University in Hillsboro earning my doctorate in Occupational Therapy. Theo recovered from his hand injury because of a hand therapist, so I will be giving back by furthering my studies into hand therapy. I will do this in honor of Theo Hall who gave me confidence a long time ago at the senior class prom—confidence, just like Claire's nail polish slogan."

- Fred Freemark

"I went to high school with Theo and Claire and was jealous of Theo for his popularity and skill at playing the violin. I tripped him and almost caused him and Claire to slide into an oncoming school bus—risking their lives and destroying Theo's violin hand. They sentenced me to prison for five years for assault and attempted manslaughter. I learned a huge lesson in prison. My arrogance and selfishness were entirely of my making. I want to atone for my actions and fully support anything Theo and Claire support. They deserve my support, as I could have killed them both. I work for my father at Freemark Capitol. We buy and sell distressed companies. I have convinced my father to give back ten percent of our profits to all of Claire and Theo's causes. Also, I'd like to publicly apologize to Ashley Rich for being such an ass at the senior class prom."

- Nadia Jama

"The Lake Oswego Progressive Church of America took my family in as refugees from Ethiopia when I was five. They accepted my family as if we were their own. My family endured racial discrimination beyond belief in America. Republican right-wing animals nearly killed my father. Lake Oswego Progressive Church of America's decision to turn their property into a refugee resettlement home was brilliant. I want to thank them for giving me the responsibility of being its manager. Every day of my life is a blessing to help others find acceptance and love in Portland. The Lake Oswego Progressive Church of America and Lizzy, the wonder dog, helped me and my family assimilate into American culture. My family owes our lives to this congregation. To give back, I have convinced our mosque to contribute to the refugee resettlement home as long as it exists."

- Emily Young

"It's an honor to be here. Thanks to Theo and Claire, Stage Fright Cosmetics was born. Theo's encouragement in high school led me to Reed College and the idea of starting a cosmetics company that provides earth-friendly products. Claire's fame has made our company into what it is today. Our company has been giving back ten percent of our profits to Emily's Wish, and we'll continue to do so indefinitely."

- Marty Steinfeld

"I went to Curtis with Theo, dropped out, got a job as a bus driver, and tried to kill myself. Theo came to my apartment in the nick of time. I was pointing a gun at myself when Theo showed up. He kept me from pulling the trigger. Later, I contacted Dr. Dawson, and we worked out some issues that I have, that got to the heart of the problem. My prescription antidepressants were just the opposite of what I needed; they made me gain weight and, ironically, suicidal. I'll be giving back by supporting the Trevor Project, the world's largest youth suicide prevention and crisis intervention nonprofit. Ben helped me discover that my sexual preference/orientation was causing me emotional pain."

- Harold Sweeny

"Theo used to work for me at McDanny's near Portland State University for about a month. I read all about him in the news and had to come today to apologize publicly for how I treated him. I asked Theo to apologize to a customer who falsely accused Theo of swearing at him. Theo did the right thing and didn't compromise his integrity by apologizing to the belligerent customer. I now own ten McDanny's franchises. I'll support Emma's wish, as the homeless population near many of our restaurants need help. From the inspiration of Stage Fright Cosmetics, I'll be giving back by donating ten percent of my profits to the Emma's Wish foundation."

- Janet Devine (Claire's mother)

"I was wrong about Claire, this church, and many other things. The Lake Oswego Fundamentalist Church of America taught lies to me. I thought that money and status were the most important things in life. Through the character displayed by Claire, her friends, Dr. Dawson, this church, and many others, they all believed that my bigotry, homophobia, and religious fundamentalism could be overcome. I've started attending the Lake Oswego Progressive Church of America. I've discovered that every human being should have the freedom to express themselves—as Dr. Martin Luther King said, "by the content of their character rather than the color of their skin," and as I would add, their sexual preference. Don't forget, Clair, if it weren't for me, you wouldn't have wanted to match your nail polish color with your outfits. Since seeing the vision that Claire, her friends, and associates have, I'll be giving back, by supporting all of Claire's causes and I will do whatever I can to support this wonderfully progressive church."

- Palmer Grandstone

"I've known Alexandria Savich since we played in the Boston Youth Philharmonic. My family has owned Grandstone Galleries in Boston, Massachusetts, for three generations. I've been a self-centered narcissist for most of my life, nearly destroying everyone who came into my path for my gain. When I did community service for six months, I made an enormous change. I attempted to kill a barking dog next door to me. They arrested me and assigned me to a local dog park in Boston to pick up dog feces   for my attempted auctions. It humiliated me beyond belief. This abandoned dog I hold in my hands taught me a life lesson. Floppy was alone, scared, hungry, and abandoned—like many people. We bonded. I never took care of anyone or anything in my entire life. Floppy changed my life. Thousands of dogs, like Floppy, are alone, scared, hungry, and abandoned. I'll be giving back, by supporting The American Society for the Prevention of Cruelty to Animals, with a percentage of all my profits at my store going to them and giving back by supporting the Emma's Wish Foundation to help alone, scared, hungry, and abandoned people on our streets."

- Emma Hall

"Palmer, it will never cease to amaze me where you got that weird accent. Someday perhaps you could explain it to us.

In any case, my brother, Theo, is an inspiration. He's been to hell and back. I've been relatively lucky. Since everything is online these days, NASA has allowed me to live here in Portland and work remotely on the James Webb Space Telescope. Nothing would make me happier than living in the same town as my family. Oh Theo, I saw you sneak in and out of my planetarium show at OMSI a decade ago. I let Ben know you were at least in Portland. This helped them narrow down their search. As stupid as you were to live in Tent City, Blast would never have happened without the out-of-tune train horn and your hand injury. I'm so proud to be your sister. I will give back by working with the profit-making companies that are part of the James Webb Space Telescope program to give back some of their profits to the Oregon Museum of Science and Industry that inspires young people to pursue careers in science. I will also give back by donating money from my personal income to Emma's Wish. Thomas, my stepfather, named Emma's Wish after me, I'm so flattered. How cool is that?"

- Theo Hall

"Most of you know me as the guy who used his violin case to stop a mass shooter. Previously, I was directly involved in being homeless while living in Tent City. From this experience, my symphonic work, Blast, is in three movements, Addiction, Treatment, and Recovery. I will give back by supporting the Hazelden Betty Ford Foundation that works toward Addiction and Mental Health Treatment. Gun violence is another issue that I've been directly involved in, as you all know. I want to give back to the Coalition to Stop Gun Violence. Of course, Emma's Wish will also get my never ending support. I learned valuable lessons in life from my arm injury that there's more to life than fame, money, or success. The love and support of my family, friends, and humankind take precedence over everything."

- April Dawson

"I attend Lake Oswego Grade School. I'm ten years old. We have an orchestra program that Ms. Van Pelt teaches. She told us all about Theo Hall. He plays the violin better than anyone except for my mother. I play the violin too. Ms. Van Pelt let me touch the violin

Theo played in school. It was the most thrilling day of my life. Theo stopped a mass shooter in New York, plays the violin in the New York Philharmonic, the finest orchestra in the world, and wrote a major symphony. I love Theo. I want to be just like him. He's my hero."

After the clapping stops, I say, "Theo, your face is the color of Claire's red nail polish."

- Claire Devine

"April, Theo is my hero too. I've loved him since I was your age. Palmer, I would also like to know where you got your strange accent. Most of you know me or have heard of me. I'm an actress on Evenings of our Lives and the co-owner of Stage Fright Cosmetics, which has contributed millions of dollars to Emma's Wish. Theo and I want to partner with you to do something good for the world. You are all here because you have shown an interest in making your spheres of the world better. Besides giving back to Emma's Wish, my biggest issue is women's rights because of the struggle I've had in the movie business and several close calls I've had with physical violence against women. I want to give back even more to the National Organization for Women and help women learn how to defend themselves. Additionally, I owe my life to Belle Brown, a self-defense instructor at the Portland Police Training Facility."

Belle stands, and everyone claps.

- Palmer stands

"Just as Theo seems to be everyone's hero, William F. Buckley was my hero. I listened to every syllable of, what I thought at the time, his brilliant selfishness. He turned me into a selfish person much the same as Ayn Rand, another one of my former heroes. Again, little Floppy changed all this. I've discarded the philosophy of selfishness, but my accent would be hard to discard."

I conclude with this, "Thank you all for coming today. I hope that you will all be inspired by the Give Back Initiative and contribute to causes that are dear to your hearts. Thanks to Theo and Claire for their leadership using their national celebrity to help make this world a more compassionate place for everyone. Please join us for a reception in the lower level."

62. Balloons

We stare at a letter addressed to us from Universal Studios. It reads:

Dear Theo Hall and Claire Devine,

Alexandria Savich gave me your address. She's a friend, as we both attended St. Olaf College together. My talent scouts have been following your careers for several years. We're aware of the recent blockbuster movie that Weiner Films wanted to shoot. The parent company of Weiner Films gave us the rights to produce it. Because of Ms. Devine's exceptional talent, fame, and on-screen charisma, we would like to offer her the starring role as initially planned. Also, because of the rave reviews and movie score feel of Mr. Hall's debut of his symphony, "Blast," we would like to ask him to write the score for the movie. Please contact my office to negotiate this multi-million-dollar contract at your earliest convenience. If you accept our offer, a healthy advance of one million dollars apiece will hopefully entice both of you to join us.

Sincerely, Blanch Bucherand, Chairperson, Universal Studios

P.S. Alex told me about your "Give Back Initiative." Because of this inspiration from both of you, the board of Universal Studios has voted unanimously to donate ten percent of its profits to Emma's Wish. Like both of you, and in honor of Theo's twin sister, Emma, we would also like to be a partner in ending homelessness in the entire country. If Stage Fright Cosmetics can give ten percent profits to fix this problem, we can too.

We both sit at the kitchen table and stare at each other.

Claire looks at me and says, "Hey Theo, we need to go on a walk."

"Why?" I ask.

"Because that's why. We both must wear our cargo pants too."

"Cargo pants? Mine are all stained from Tent City. I haven't worn them for years."

"All the more reason to wear them. I'll take my tiger claw, just in case."

"Should I bring my violin case?"

"Nah, you don't need it with me to protect you."

"Where are we going?"

"It's a surprise."

We live in a high rise in Portland's South Waterfront District. Our condo has an insane view of the Willamette River. Just take the elevator down to the main floor, and there's a fabulous park, various eateries, and the light rail will take us downtown in minutes. Claire's company, Stage Fright Cosmetics, has blessed us with the resources to live here, and the royalties from Blast are tremendous. It was strange to resign from the New York Philharmonic. People thought I was nuts, but composing music pushes all my buttons. Besides, I can live in Portland near the people who love me. Claudia was right about this one. Family is more important than everything.

We walk past the park, all green from the Portland rain, and go to a coffee shop.

"Claire, I remember when Johnny Accardo bought me a cup of coffee here. He bought it because I looked like I was living on the street—which I was."

"Theo, let's go."

"Where?"

"You'll see."

With coffee in hand, we walk toward the red balloon sculpture and sit on the bench that looks at it and the Tilikum Crossing. This high-tech bridge only allows bikes, pedestrians, and the light rail—no cars. I think this is cool.

"This is a very famous bench, Claire. I sat here with Johnny Accardo when we bumped into each other on the tram. He had cancer. He pretended that his memory was gone but told Ben he had met me on the tram. Ben knew I was living somewhere in Tent City. Unfortunately, he didn't find out until after my assault."

"What else is this bench famous for?" Claire asks me.

"This is the bench where Alex asked Ben to marry him."

"Well, now we're getting down to brass tacks," Claire says.

I wonder where this is going.

"Theo, do you remember when you said you didn't feel in a 'family way' with Claudia?"

"Yep."

"Do you feel the same way about me?"

"Nope."

"Will you marry me?"

"Do I have any other choice?"

"Absolutely not. Remember, I'm the one with the tiger claw. Mess with me, and you'll pay."

"How much?" I ask.

"Kiss me, Theo."

"Is that a wish or a command?"

"Both."

About The Author

The Rev. Dr. James Asparro is a retired U.S. Navy Chaplain who deployed in the Western Pacific several times during the cold war and served as a navy chaplain with the fleet Marines. He was stationed stateside, in Iceland, and on sea duty in the Mediterranean. He has worked as a chaplain at Oregon State Hospital, Linfield College, and in the VA Health Care System. He was the pastor of an American Baptist church for four years before going on active duty with the navy. He holds degrees from University of Portland, Yale Divinity School, and Claremont School of Theology.

To contact him and find out more about his books visit:

www.jamesasparro.com

About The Book

If you have enjoyed this book. Please consider reading the prequels to it: Salt of the Earth a Portland Story and Obsessed—also written and narrated by James Asparro. Most characters in Turnaround have colorful backgrounds encapsulated in the prequels. New characters emerge in Turnaround to keep the story fresh and exciting.

Sound effects in the Audible version of this book were both recorded by the author and purchased royalty free from Envato Elements.

Made in the USA
Coppell, TX
10 October 2024

38463758R00125